Life
Unexpected
Book One

Safe In
His Arms

MDSnitker

Psalm 55:22

Melanie D. Snitker

Cover: Blue Valley Author Services
www.bluevalleyauthorservices.com

ISBN-10: 0-9975289-1-5
ISBN-13: 978-0-9975289-1-6

CONTENTS

v

You came near when I called you,
and you said, "Do not fear."
O Lord, you took up my case;
you redeemed my life.
Lamentations 3:57-58

Chapter One

Anna Henderson took in a steadying breath and blew it back out again. After navigating the maze that was Dallas/Fort Worth, the smaller town of Quintin, Texas seemed downright tame.

The Dodge van rolled to a stop at a red light, punctuated by a whine from the passenger seat.

"Hang on, Epic. We'll be there in a few minutes." Her Great Pyrenees had been patient the last few hours of the drive, but he was getting antsy. She sympathized as she flexed her ankles to keep the blood flowing in her legs.

When they'd left Utah two days ago, Anna had no idea where she was going. She only knew she had to get as far away as possible.

She still smelled the acrid smoke and remembered the way the fire heated her skin. The panic that plagued her since she'd realized her ex-boyfriend, Liam, had seen her through the flames kept her moving.

Until she drove into Quintin.

Within moments, peace enveloped her. It was something she'd sorely lacked for longer than she cared to admit and impossible to ignore.

"I think this will be a good place for us, Epic. But it'll take a while to get everything figured out."

They'd sat in the parking lot of a grocery store for a half hour while Anna perused the city map she'd picked up. That's when she saw it. A shopping center bordered on one side by a large city park. It was as if a light had shone on the map from above, accompanied by a chorus of singing. Slight exaggeration, but yeah.

Perfect.

Now she was sitting at a stoplight, the map open on her lap. The light turned green. She needed to merge and raised herself up in the driver's seat. Despite her attempt, she couldn't see the passenger mirror through the white fringe.

"Epic! Lie down!"

He groaned as the top of his head sank low enough for her to see. His body hung off the side and front of the seat.

"We're almost there."

Anna maneuvered her van through a series of streets towards the park. She flipped her right blinker on as she slowed and then halted at a stop sign. Epic stood again and pressed his wet nose against the window.

When it was her turn, she steered her vehicle into the entrance. Exactly as the map had suggested, the park bordered a shopping center that included a large bookstore and numerous independent shops. In fact, the parking lots for both were separated by only a thin strip of grass.

The clouds to the west took on an orange hue as the sun sank below the horizon. It was Monday, the last day of February. Tomorrow was the start of a new month and, she hoped, a new chapter in her life.

Anna's stomach rumbled. Other than chips and a piece of fruit, she'd eaten little. Putting as much distance between her and Liam was the priority. She looked forward to stopping tonight and having something more substantial to eat. But before she did anything else, there was no doubt Epic had business to take care of. She eyed the public restrooms not far away and made a mental note.

She claimed a parking space and turned the engine off. A few moments of observation and she was confident they were alone.

After shoving her keys into her jeans, she proceeded to the van's door and slid it open. Epic traversed the distance from van to pavement with no effort, his giant tongue lolling out of his mouth. He shook out his heavy white fur, pieces flying into the air as they caught the fading sunshine.

Anna clipped a leash to his red collar. Epic lifted his head and stretched out his neck as he ran his wet tongue across her chin. "You're welcome. Let's stretch our legs."

She adjusted the windbreaker around her, shoved a tennis ball into the pocket, and led Epic to the grass where he could take care of business. Once he was done and she'd cleaned up after him, Anna took off jogging down the path. It was a moderate pace for her while Epic merely loped. As they ran, some of the tension that'd been building since they left Utah fell away.

The park was quiet and the sky darkened. The first star peered down on them as the cool air grew crisp. Out here, it ought to be easy to forget the past.

If only it were that simple.

She tossed a glimpse over her shoulder to ensure no one was around. At the moment, she couldn't imagine a time when danger didn't lurk around every corner.

Whenever she was in a crowd, she half expected Liam to be standing there. Thinking about the possibility made her shiver. And to think she'd trusted him. If he ever found her…

No.

Anna had to focus on creating a new life. Liam wouldn't find her here. She'd collected her meager savings, paid cash for the old Dodge van, and was using a throwaway phone. She intended on staying invisible.

And she wasn't going to trust anyone. Certainly not blindly like she had Liam.

She heaved a sigh and slowed her pace. There wasn't a soul around. She removed Epic's leash and threw the tennis ball as far as she could into the field.

With more grace than one would expect from a dog his size, Epic turned in mid-air and bounded off after it. He scooped the ball up off the grass and it disappeared into his massive mouth.

Even though he was perfectly capable of crushing the ball, Epic dropped it at her feet in the same condition he found it, albeit slimier, each time.

They continued their game of fetch for another twenty minutes before Epic wandered and took care of more business.

She checked the time on her phone. Almost

seven. She whistled for Epic and he joined her in moments. "Come on, we need to make dinner before it gets much later."

As if Epic understood every word, he leaned forward and grasped the end of the leash with his mouth. Without hesitating, he led his owner back to the van.

Another survey of the area assured her they were still alone. She pulled out a two-gallon bucket and filled it with fresh water for Epic. She poured a bowl full of dog food. He appeared grateful and began to eat. Anna got lunchmeat, a cheese square, and bread out of the cooler. Sandwich time. Again.

Anna took a large bite and chewed thoughtfully. Most of the ice in the cooler had melted. She'd need to get more in the morning.

She swallowed. "Don't worry, buddy. I'm gonna find a job tomorrow. I'll get us out of this mess." The dog watched her and tilted his head sideways. "I'm serious. Wait and see." She eyed the sandwich in her hand. "I'm ready to eat something else here soon." Epic seemed perplexed before returning to his own food. "Okay, I admit, it could be worse. How about we both upgrade? I'll get something better and you can have my sandwiches."

Anna rubbed the dog's head. The combination of her short stature and the mammoth size of the dog meant she didn't have to bend down to reach him.

When they'd finished, she turned the van on long enough to charge her cell phone. The heater filled the interior with warmth until Anna started to sweat. It would be enough until they fell asleep. It was dark outside except for the lights around the shopping center.

"Well, there's nothing left to do but get some rest."

Epic knew the process and moved out of the way while Anna dragged the comforters out of the back of the van. She turned the engine off, locked all of the doors, and stretched out on the middle seat. With the blankets tucked under her chin, she watched as Epic squeezed himself into the space at the floorboard and curled up on the edge of the comforter that had reached the floor.

The full-sized, dark green van might be old and the seats torn, but it was roomy enough for the two of them.

Anna draped her arm over the side of the seat and reached for the cylinder attached to Epic's collar. She felt the cool metal against her fingers and thought about the thumb drive inside. A few towns back, she'd stopped at a library to use their computer. But the files wouldn't open and it said they were encrypted. She hoped that meant they could be decrypted somehow.

She needed help. It was possible that drive contained the evidence she needed to get Liam out of her life forever.

Epic groaned as he settled in for the night. Anna tucked her hand under the blankets.

It didn't matter how uncertain life was, Epic made her feel safe. Any measure of security counted for a whole lot when it came to sleeping in a strange town.

Liam pulled keys out of his pocket and

rummaged through them until he found the one that would unlock Anna's door. She'd hesitated when he suggested she give him a key to her apartment. But he'd insisted, accusing her of not trusting him.

He entered the space and turned the lights on. She'd left almost everything behind except for a selection of clothing, a few personal items, and that stupid dog of hers.

This was the third time he'd come in here, hoping to find some kind of clue showing him where she might be headed.

And again, there was nothing.

Not even on that blasted computer of hers.

Liam shoved the monitor off her desk. It landed on the floor with a satisfying crash. The monitor rested on its side and he knocked it over the rest of the way with his foot for good measure.

That fire was supposed to be a foolproof plan to take care of his failing business and make Anna pay for walking away from him. All evidence should've burned in that building along with everything else.

He'd watched Anna as the place filled with smoke. The last thing he'd expected was for her to grab the thumb drive and have enough sense to get out of the building before it fell down around her.

That blasted drive! Liam shoved Anna's rolling chair against her desk. He needed to get it back and destroy it before she found a way to recover the files.

She might have slipped away from him, but he was going to find her, one way or another.

⋞ ❤ ⋟

Anna had set her phone alarm for eight in the

morning. It turned out to be unnecessary. The moment the sun brightened the sky, Epic awakened her by licking her hand.

The cold morning air bit at her face and she struggled with which would be worse: Lie there and continue to freeze, or brave the temperature long enough to turn the heater on.

Epic's insistence made her mind up for her and she moved to the driver's seat with a shiver.

The temperature gauge climbed slowly. She turned the heater on high. The warmth flowed over her and she lounged on the middle seat again.

Epic whined at the door but she shook her head. "It won't kill you to wait ten minutes." He followed her with his big brown eyes, the air from the heater whipping the hair on his face around. Anna giggled. "You're in serious need of a haircut." She ran her fingers through her own and realized the tresses nearly reached the middle of her back. She could use a trim, too.

Over the next hour, they went through what had become their morning routine. Bathroom breaks, breakfast of dry cereal for her and dog food for Epic, followed by an early morning run in the park.

A while later, Anna drove to a nearby truck stop and parked the van. She wrinkled her nose, not overly impressed with the place.

She was in desperate need of a shower. Her appearance hadn't exactly been a priority over the last few days. But she had every intention of securing a job before the sun set again. And she couldn't do that when she smelled just like her dog.

With a deep breath, she gave Epic a pat, and made her way across the parking lot and inside.

Fifteen minutes later, hot water removed the grime from her trip and carried it to the drain. Too bad her past wasn't as easy to wash away.

Wiping the steam off the mirror, Anna peered at her reflection. Six months ago, she appeared younger than her twenty-three years. But now... Dark circles colored the skin below her eyes and she felt like she'd aged. Liam had done a number on her. In more ways than one. She pulled up the sleeve of her shirt and took in the fading yellow bruises. Memories of the way he'd grabbed her arm made her flinch.

Anna shook her head in an attempt to banish all thoughts of Liam. She focused on applying concealer and a touch of blush. She wasn't much for makeup, but you do what you've got to do. And after what she'd been through the last couple of weeks, it didn't hurt.

Anna had a plan. She needed to get a job and make enough money to afford an apartment before the weather got warm. It was okay for Epic to stay in the van for a few hours at a time now. But another month and the temperature would be too warm.

Time was ticking and as the sand emptied from the hourglass, it added weight to the pressure building on her shoulders.

"You'll never make it on your own, Anna. Not without me. You're nothing without me."

Liam's gravelly voice echoed in her head and she flinched. There was a time she might have believed him. She rolled her shoulders back.

"You're wrong, Liam. I can do this."

She finished getting cleaned up and then headed back, hoping her van was still where she left it. If she decided to take up residence in Quintin, she'd have to find a nicer truck stop.

Just over two hours later, Anna positioned the van under a tree in the lot nearest the park. She made sure Epic's water bucket was full, gave him a good scratch behind the ears, and kissed his nose. "Be a good boy. And wish me luck, huh?"

Epic raised his giant head and let out a low woof.

Anna grinned. "Thanks. I'll see you in a while. Behave yourself."

She hopped out of the van and locked the doors. It was better safe than sorry. Though anyone who tried to break into the van would get the scare of a lifetime in the form of a giant white carpet with teeth.

She brushed stray hairs off her jeans, straightened her shirt, and headed towards the shopping center.

It was almost noon and there were several restaurants. The trick was to find the one that seemed to be the busiest during lunch hour.

It didn't take long. The revolving door of one establishment caught her attention. The sign sported a burger and the words, "J's Parkview Diner."

Anna turned and held her hand above her eyes to block the sun. Yep, her van was still visible.

"Okay, it's time to make a good impression."

With a deep breath, she squared her shoulders. The next time the door swung open, she ducked inside. She wasn't sure what she'd expected from the diner. Greasy walls, maybe? A dirty floor?

Instead, a sparkling clean dining area with booths and tables reminiscent of a fifties diner greeted her from the doorway. Customers occupied most of the tables, busy eating their meals. She noticed the place hyped made-to-order burgers. Her mouth watered at the thought. They even had homemade milkshakes.

Her eyes roved the place, landing on one man behind the counter. He stood tall and thin. Anna guessed him to be in his mid- to late-twenties. She imagined classmates teased him for his skinny stature when he was a kid. He maintained an air of confidence about him as he handled the flood of customers. Not only that, but he met each one of them with a greeting.

There was something about his smile that drew her in. Maybe it was the way his eyes crinkled at the corners. No matter who he spoke to, the smile seemed genuine.

Anna had noticed several people who worked at the diner, but it was that guy she decided she'd speak with first. Getting in line with the customers, she waited her turn.

When he shifted his attention to her, his brown eyes held her own. She noticed that some of his brown hair almost reached his eyebrows, one of which lifted as he waited for her response to a question she must not have heard.

"What can I get you?"

Peering up — and up — at his face, Anna stood as tall as possible and spoke. "You can give me a job."

He motioned towards the line of customers behind her. "We're right in the middle of lunch hour."

"And from what I'm seeing, you could use more help." She refused to drop her gaze, even though he seemed to try to garner more from her than she was willing to reveal. "If you'll direct me to your manager. Or the owner…"

A corner of his mouth lifted at the same time a sparkle of amusement lit his eyes. "You're talking to both."

Chapter Two

Joel Ash watched as a hint of surprise marched across the small gal's face before she schooled her features. Telling her he needed no more help wouldn't be true. But during lunch hour... well, he didn't have time to deal with it right now.

Instead of leaving, she pierced him with green eyes the same shade as the lettuce in one of the ingredient bins. When he realized she wasn't going anywhere, he made a quick decision. "Come back when things quiet down." He expected her to leave.

Instead, she ordered lunch. "I'll take a burger with cheddar, lettuce, tomato, and mustard. A side of your seasoned fries. Oh, and water. Please."

Joel picked up a plate and fixed her burger as she requested. He added a generous helping of seasoned fries. His diner was famous for the oversized burgers and he doubted the small woman could consume half of one. "Would you like a chocolate chip, sugar, or oatmeal raisin cookie?"

"Cookies come with the meal?" She seemed

surprised.

He shrugged "Why not? Adults like dessert, too. I don't see why most restaurants only give it out to kids."

"Chocolate chip, please."

After she paid the cashier, he handed the plate to her along with a napkin and a plastic knife. She took them and her water cup. Joel offered her a parting smile and turned his attention to the next customer in line.

More than once during the lunch rush, Joel noticed the woman sitting at one of the smallest tables he offered. She'd finished maybe half of her burger and wrapped the rest of it up in a napkin. Unlike the majority of his customers, he never saw her playing on her cell phone.

Things finally quieted down. When he had a few minutes, he made his way across the dining area. She faced the window, her attention focused on the park beyond. Her dark-colored hair hung to the middle of her back. Subtle waves caught the light from the window and created blond accents. Her chin rested in her palm. He noted the crease of worry between her brows.

She must've heard his approach and became instantly alert, clasping her hands and laying them on the table in front of her. "Your diner makes an excellent burger."

"Thank you. It's the shining star of the menu." His burgers had made his place famous. Well, famous in Quintin, anyway. He slid into the bench seat opposite her and smiled. "You want a job. What brought you into my diner?"

She remained serious, her eyes darting to the

front door every time it opened. Was she expecting someone else?

"Your steady stream of customers. And the fact that there's always a high turnover rate in the food industry."

That was true. Although he prided himself on keeping employees much longer than normal. But one of his best had quit several days before. "What's your name?"

"Anastasia Henderson. But call me Anna." She stuck a hand out. "And you are?"

He grasped her hand in his own and gave it a firm shake, her skin frigid. The temptation to hold her hand longer in order to warm it surprised him. "Joel Ash."

When he released her hand, she used it to brush some hair behind her ear. "You own this place?"

"Yep." Joel admired the girl's spunk. But Anastasia? He swore her name was longer than she was tall. But it fit her. He would have guessed her to be college age because of her appearance, but suspected she might be older than that. "Why do you want to work here?"

She shrugged. "It's a long story."

Okay. What did that mean? "And are you wanting short-term or long-term employment?"

Anastasia fingered a section of her hair and absently wrapped it around a finger. "I'm hoping for long-term. But none of us can see the future."

"That's true." Joel studied her a moment. He prided himself on being able to read people and usually got a sense of the person's character within moments.

But Anastasia here was an enigma. Everything

from the way she held herself to how she met him head-on spoke of self-assurance. But there was something else there, hidden right below the surface. A vulnerability that bordered on sadness. Or maybe fear. Was she scared of him? Surely not.

He slipped his right hand into his pocket, his fingers grazing the wooden handle of his pocket knife. Something told Joel to give her the job. He'd learned long ago to trust his instincts. "Hours are nine to six with an hour for lunch and two fifteen-minute breaks. I expect a lot from my employees."

"I'm a hard worker. That won't be a problem. Do any meals come with the job?"

Joel expected her to indicate she was joking, but her expression remained deadpan. "Are you negotiating?" Her chin rose slightly. "I'll throw in a burger and fries at lunch."

She was good. "Deal."

"You're something else." Joel shook his head and swallowed back his amusement. "Don't make me regret this."

"You won't." Her eyes were serious as they held his own. "Thank you."

"You're welcome." Joel put his palms on the table and pushed himself up. "Let me go grab paperwork for you to fill out and then we'll go over a few things."

When he returned, she was watching out the window again. She slowly turned her attention to him and reached for the papers.

"I'll be back when you've got those filled out."

Anastasia wrote on the white sheets in front of her. Joel kept plenty busy getting things caught up after the lunch rush. His gaze flitted towards the woman as she attacked the paperwork with determination.

When she finished, he rejoined her and told her she'd be working Tuesday through Saturday. The diner closed for business Sunday and Monday.

"That sounds great." Anastasia folded her hands and rested them on the table. "For my lunch and breaks, I'll need to do quick errands in the area. But I'll be back before my time is up." She paused. "Are you serious about the burger and fries?"

"You get one free meal each shift. But if I catch you abusing it, the privilege will be revoked." Her brows rose. "It's happened before, as crazy as that sounds."

"What was someone doing? Sneaking fries all day?"

"More like taking a bag full of burgers home in the evening."

"Yikes. Yeah, that's not cool." Anastasia offered him a ghost of a smile that didn't quite reach her eyes. "You won't have to worry about that. One burger's good enough for me." She picked up the leftovers she'd wrapped from lunch.

"I'll hold you to it." Joel glanced through the paperwork and noticed that one line remained blank. "You forgot to put your address on here."

Anastasia chewed on her bottom lip. "I just got into town. I don't have a permanent address yet. As soon as I do, I'll update you."

He wanted to ask what hotel she was staying in but bit his tongue. He had her cell phone number, and that was all he needed for now.

They were silent a moment before Anastasia cleared her throat. "When do I start?"

"Be here tomorrow morning. Nine o'clock sharp."

She extended her hand to him. "I'll see you then."

This time, when his hand closed over her much smaller one, energy traveled from there, up his arm, and straight to his heart.

He only nodded once and watched as she left his diner. Another glance at the paperwork confirmed what he'd suspected: She was twenty-three, four years younger than himself. The only thing she'd listed under past employment was secretary. Nothing specific.

Confident in his decision to hire the woman, he was as certain that there was a lot more to Anastasia Henderson than met the eye.

Joel glanced at the clock on the wall. It was almost one-thirty. He grabbed a waiting to-go box, jogged to his car, and drove to the family hair salon a couple miles away.

Brooke was sitting on the curb out front when he arrived. She stood and approached him. "I was wondering if you weren't coming by. I'm starving."

Joel handed the box to his friend. "Sorry I'm late. I had someone come in asking about a job. Since Sam quit last week, I've been short-handed." Joel leaned against a pole supporting the awning above the sidewalk. "I came over as soon as I hired her."

Brooke swallowed the fry she was eating. "Her? Is she pretty?"

"Are you serious?" Brooke was forever trying to set him up on a date with someone. No matter who it was. "My employees are off limits." He was only half joking.

"I know. Relax." She offered him a fry and he

declined with a shake of his head. "I called the mechanic and my car should be ready by the end of the day. Thanks for bringing lunch out."

"You're welcome. Is Chess still planning on picking you up and taking you to get it?"

"Yes. I'm sure glad it was a simple fix."

Joel was, too. He, Brooke, and Chess were all friends who bought a house together. Being roommates came in especially handy during instances like this when one of them needed help.

Brooke was watching him, a playful half-smile on her face. "Come on, Joel. Is she pretty? You shouldn't discount her just because she's an employee." Her eyes remained on Joel as she took a large bite out of her burger.

Joel pictured the way Anastasia appeared as she gazed out his diner window. He could still see the moment she turned those green eyes on him. "Yeah, she's pretty."

"You should ask her out."

"No." Dating an employee was never a good idea. Besides, he had enough on his plate right now without adding to it. He shoved thoughts of his parents from his mind. After spending his teen years in the foster care system, Joel grew to appreciate the times in his life when things were going smoothly. Like now. Why fix what wasn't broken?

As beautiful as Anastasia might be, the last thing he needed was to throw a wrench in the works.

Liam eyed Anna's Toyota. He delivered a hard kick to the bumper. He'd been driving down Oak

Street when he spotted her vehicle in a lot of used cars for sale. It was a stroke of dumb luck, but he'd take it.

The car dealer held up a hand. "Please, sir. Easy."

"Right, right. Well, the woman who sold this vehicle to you had no right to do so. She's my little sister and she's running away. I'm worried for her health. Her life." Liam wiped at the corner of his eye, feigning tears. "I'm trying to locate her. I need to bring her home and get her the help she needs."

The dealer's eyes widened. "I'm sorry. I didn't know. I gave her a fair trade-in price."

Liam stilled. "She traded this vehicle in? For what? If you give me the description and license plate number, I can track her down."

"Of course." The dealer motioned Liam to follow him. "She paid in cash. I'm not sure how much information I have. But if you'll come with me, I'll check the computer."

"I appreciate that." Liam tapped his chin with a knuckle as anticipation filled him. This was the first lead he'd had since she disappeared. *You can run, Anna. But I* will *find you.*

Epic snatched the half of a hamburger out of the air, chewed twice, and swallowed. Big, brown eyes watched her and his massive tail swooped back and forth.

"I told you I'd get a job today, boy." Anna tossed him a cold fry. "We'll have one hot meal every day. Give me a month, and we'll find somewhere else to live. We can do this for a month, can't we?"

Epic's eyes followed the fries as she lobbed them into the air one by one. When the last fry disappeared, he moved to sit at her feet by a picnic table in the park.

Anna shifted until her back rested against the edge of the table. Epic closed his eyes and licked his chops. Content without a worry in the world.

She wondered if she'd ever feel that way again. And when she did, how would she know it was true? Lasting? She'd been fooled before.

Anna thought back to the first time she'd met Liam. It seemed like a lifetime ago. At twenty, she'd been on her own for three years after her grandparents died. She bounced from part-time job to part-time job and she didn't always have a place to stay.

She and Liam had both been waiting at the same bus stop when they began to talk. He was starting up an advertising agency and claimed she had the perfect phone voice. He offered her a job as the secretary on the spot and she couldn't turn it down. Not when work had been inconsistent at best.

Anna had thanked her lucky stars. It'd gotten her enough money to get a tiny apartment and the job was stable. She couldn't have asked for more. Liam might've been demanding as an employer but she hadn't complained.

And it worked well for two years. That's when Liam showed an interest in her that went beyond that of an employee. He'd always been the flattering type and when he turned his charm on her, she fell for it. She frowned. Thinking back, she couldn't believe how clueless she'd been.

Anna was thankful for this new job at the diner.

But it didn't mean she'd trust her boss or anyone else further than she could throw them. Things would be simpler that way. Safer.

She and Epic spent their evening soaking in the last of the sun before it set and left them going inside the van for the night.

Anna hadn't been asleep long before the dream began.

Flames licked the walls of the building, consuming everything they touched. Anna backed away. Her hand searched for the doorknob she knew was right behind her. Becoming frantic, she turned to find nothing but solid wall.

Heat from the flames singed her arms as they closed in. Precious oxygen disappeared and smoke choked her lungs.

All the while, Liam watched from a distance, a sneer stretching his mouth unnaturally wide.

Anna jolted upright, the comforter slipping off her body and landing on top of Epic. Despite the cold air, sweat made her clothing cling to her skin. She shivered and stamped down any memory of the dream — the same dream that had haunted her since she left Utah.

Epic rested his chin on her hand and whined.

"I'm okay, buddy." She lay on the bench seat again, her cheek against Epic's warm head. He bathed her hand with his large, warm tongue.

Anna purposefully slowed her breathing and tried to relax. She focused on memories of her grandparents. The way her grandpa would light his tobacco pipe as he set a chessboard up for them to play. The hours she spent with her grandma in the kitchen baking and chatting about their day.

They'd raised her since she was a toddler. They'd made her childhood a happy one.

Then Grandpa passed when she was fifteen, and Grandma two years later.

She had no other family left. And rather than go into the foster care system for a year, she'd set out on her own.

That seemed like a lifetime ago now.

"I wish you were here. I miss you both."

"Give it to God, Anna. He'll see you through."

Grandma always had such faith. Anna had lost sight of that once Liam came into her life. She'd put her trust in a man who seemed to be the answer to all of her problems.

Anna concentrated on the nights when she was a child and her grandparents would listen as she said her prayers before bed. She'd gone to sleep safe. Loved.

For the first time in years, Anna let a silent prayer flow from her heart. She thanked God for her new job and asked for safety until she drifted off to sleep once more.

Chapter Three

Joel stepped through the front door of his home. Talk about a long day. He'd hired Anastasia, taken lunch to Brooke, then come back to find the mail had arrived with information he'd been waiting on.

A building had opened in the Dallas/Ft. Worth area about forty minutes from Quintin. After multiple nudgings from customers and his friends, Joel was considering opening a second diner location.

If it did half as well as this one, Joel would see a sizable increase in revenue.

It would also mean he'd be torn between the two locations. He liked to connect with his employees and customers. He didn't see how he could do either effectively if he was bouncing back and forth.

Joel had an appointment to tour the site on Saturday and hopefully that would help in the decision-making process.

The sounds of laughter filtered in from the

kitchen. He inhaled, the smell of chicken filling the air. Every Tuesday, they got takeout from a little place in town. Home-style chicken strips with sides of mashed potatoes and gravy, green beans, and buttered corn. Joel's stomach growled simply thinking about it.

The moment he entered the kitchen, the faces of his friends — his family — brought out a smile.

Brooke spotted him and handed him a plate. He didn't hesitate to fill it. He often ate a burger at the diner. A change in food was always welcome.

Brooke spooned beans and corn onto a plate with her chicken. She sat down at the rectangular table. "It's unusual to see you when the food's still warm, Joel."

Her comment would've annoyed him except for the humor sparkling in her eyes. She pushed her shoulder-length brown hair back and poured a generous amount of white gravy over her potatoes.

"Ha-ha. Cute." Joel sat down next to her. "How was your afternoon?"

She shrugged. "Hours of running my fingers through strangers' hair. What's not to like?"

Brooke had been a hairdresser for the last year at a family beauty shop in town. She talked about how much she liked it, but wasn't fond of the gossip that ran rampant in the place. There were times he thought she might quit and search for another form of employment. She had tenacity in spades. One thing he admired most about her.

Chess fixed his plate and took a seat next to Joel. "Nice to see you in the light of day."

"You see me Sundays and Mondays. I have a diner to run."

"That's what managers are for," Brooke said around a bite. "You have a great crew. They can get along without you once in a while."

Joel bit back a "Yes, Mom," comment. He usually stayed at the diner from nine in the morning until closing at eight. Then there was an hour of clean-up. Yes, it made for a long day, but he didn't mind. He'd always been the type to focus on one thing and put his all into it.

Even still, everyone else encouraged him to back off on the hours. But he didn't see how opening another diner would do anything but add more to his day.

Chess cleared his throat. "Brooke said you hired someone."

Joel ate a forkful of beans. "She's supposed to start tomorrow morning."

Chess dipped a chicken strip in white gravy. "Oh, I remember you talking about Sam quitting. He was good. You think she'll be able to take his place?"

"Honestly? I'm not sure. But there was something about her... I knew I had to hire her." He just hoped he hadn't made a mistake. He half expected her to not show tomorrow.

"A God thing?" Brooke raised an eyebrow.

"Yeah. A God thing."

Chess groaned. "I thought we'd agreed to leave God out of our conversations."

Silence descended on the room. Joel ran a hand over the stubble on his chin and jaw.

Religion had been a sore spot with Chess since Joel first met him. But it was Chess who kept them together, provided for them in the early days.

And they'd been relying on each other ever since.

They were the family none of them would have had otherwise.

⋙ ♥ ⋘

The next morning, Joel was relieved when Anastasia marched into the diner five minutes before nine. She was punctual and that spoke a lot about her work ethic already.

She'd pulled her hair up into a high ponytail. Joel was struck by how short she was — especially compared to him. There's no way she was any taller than five foot two.

Anastasia strode right up to the counter, back straight. "Good morning." Her brilliant eyes looked determined.

"Good morning," he greeted. A light citrus scent reached his nose. "Courtney, come up here for a moment, please?"

"Sure thing, boss." Courtney came around the corner with a paper towel in her hand. "What's up?"

"This is Anna. She'll be here in the mornings to help with prep and then stick around until six." Joel watched as the two women shook hands. "Courtney's been with me for a year now. She works mornings until noon. She knows what she's doing — at least when it comes to prep work." He winked and Courtney rolled her eyes good-naturedly. "More of the crew will arrive at ten and the manager at ten-thirty. I'll introduce you as I can."

Anastasia nodded, her eyes wide.

He motioned for her to follow him. "Come with me and I'll get your timecard set up and show you how to do that. Then I'll turn you over to Courtney."

27

Anastasia curled a section of hair around a finger while she seemed to take it all in.

"You will be one of two people responsible for prepping lunch and then again for dinner later. That includes slicing the veggies for burgers, getting salads ready, filling condiment containers, and anything else that needs to be done."

"What will I be doing during the rest of the time?"

"I'll put you on the line building burgers once you're up to speed. For the first couple of days, you can watch and see how we operate." Joel tipped his head towards the dining room. "And clean up whenever you have spare time." She looked thoughtful. "In those rare moments when you have nothing to do, I usually send the newest employee to clean out the duct work." He nodded towards the ceiling, working to keep a straight face.

Her jaw dropped a little and her gaze lifted to the panels above her. "Oh. Sure."

"I'm only teasing." She stared at him as though she weren't sure what to believe. "No cleaning out the ducts. I save that for the employees who don't show up for their shifts on time."

One corner of her mouth lifted briefly before falling again. She was taking everything way too seriously, as though her entire life depended on doing this job as close to perfect as possible. Joel didn't think she'd relaxed at all since coming in. As pretty as she was now, he could imagine what she'd look like when she smiled. He resisted the urge to put a hand on her shoulder. "This is a job and it'll keep you jumping during rushes. But there's no rule against having fun. Ask questions if you have them."

"I will. Thank you for the opportunity. You won't be sorry."

He offered an encouraging smile and left her with Courtney. He was going through paperwork when he overheard Courtney's voice in the back.

"What kind of music do you like to listen to?"

There was a pause before Anastasia's soft voice responded. "Pop. Country. I guess almost anything."

A moment later, country music played from the radio on the counter in the back. Courtney's voice promptly joined in.

When Courtney had originally asked for permission to listen to music while working on the prep, he'd agreed.

Whether it was thanks to the music or not, he didn't know, but the college student was crazy fast. And she had decent taste in music, even if her voice wasn't always on key.

In the beginning stages of putting together a business plan, Joel had been certain he wanted the diner to be a fun place for his employees to work. In his opinion, a crew that enjoyed going to work would translate into an establishment his customers not only remembered, but wanted to go back to.

It'd proven true. His people were happy to be there.

His thoughts went back to Anastasia. He didn't understand what her situation was or what brought her to his diner. But it was clear she needed this job.

There'd been more than one college student come through that Joel had taken under his wing. He had that same inclination towards Anastasia, except it was much more urgent. *I gave her a job, Lord. What else do you want me to do?*

Chapter Four

Anna's first day at the diner flew by at lightning speed. She spent both of her breaks and her entire lunch hour at the park with Epic. The cheeseburger for lunch was great and her dog concurred. It would make the sandwich at dinner much more palatable.

She met several other co-workers over the course of the day. That included Adam, one of the diner's managers. He'd been working there for less than a year but had moved into the position quickly. Anna could see why. He had a take-charge personality and everyone else respected him.

Both Adam and Joel had patiently showed her how the diner operated as the day progressed. It was still a lot to absorb.

By the time six o'clock came around, her feet ached. And to think, she'd be coming back for round two tomorrow. Truthfully, it felt good to be active and productive. She thought she preferred this over what she did at the agency.

She was clocking out for the evening when a

sound behind her brought her around. Joel gave her a reassuring smile.

"You did great today. You'll be fine here. Do you have any questions for me?"

Exhausted, Anna wasn't sure she could carry on a conversation, much less form an intelligent question. "No, I don't think so."

"Then I'll see you again tomorrow at nine?"

"Yes, I'll be here." Anna was again struck by how much taller Joel was than her. She was sure his lean stature made him seem even more so. No doubt about it, he was handsome. And those eyes...

Anna realized she was staring at his face. Heat flooded to her cheeks and she put her timecard back in its slot.

"Have a good night."

"You, too." Anna raced out of the diner. She jogged across the parking lot and smiled when she saw Epic with his nose pressed against the window of the van. The moment the door opened, he bounded out and knocked her to the ground. It was hard to protest when his tongue bathed her face and he wagged his tail excitedly.

Moments later, Epic was sniffing her pants and shirt, his nose making wet marks as he snuffled. "Oh, come on. I can't smell that bad." She lifted the neck of her shirt to her nose and grimaced. "Never mind. Let's go for a run. Then I guess it's back to the truck stop for a shower."

There were several other vehicles in the park today. Anna kept an eye out, attempting to identify which people went to which car or truck. The odds were small that Liam would track her here. The remote possibility was enough to make her blood run cold.

The sooner she saved enough money to get into an apartment or something similar, the better off they'd be. As it was, she felt the most exposed at night.

She'd much rather have more than a van separating her from everything else in the world. She could only imagine how nervous she would be, though, if not for Epic.

❧ ♥ ☙

At a new truck stop, Anna relished the hot water as it pelted against her neck and back. She washed her hair twice to get all of the grease and diner smell out. She couldn't wait to have her own place and be able to take a hot shower whenever she wanted to.

She leaned her head back into the water and rinsed the conditioner from her hair. As she wiped the water from her face, she heard the handle on the outer door jiggle.

Anna froze. She locked the door when she came in, didn't she?

Yes. She definitely locked the door. Maybe someone was checking to see if the shower was occupied. After a few minutes of listening, Anna relaxed again.

The flip-flops on her feet clung to the shower floor and made slurping noises as she turned to finish rinsing the soap off her body.

Anna turned the water off, reached for the towel she'd left on the bench nearby, and dried herself. Then she wrapped the towel around her hair.

By the time she blow dried her hair and got

dressed again, she was ready to get back to the van. A snack and sleep were in order. She stuffed her things into her duffle bag.

With the bag over one shoulder, she went through the truck stop store and exited out the double sliding doors. The air was already cooling off for the night.

Anna turned the corner of the building. A man stepped in her path without warning and she bumped into his chest.

"Excuse me, miss. Do you have any spare change?"

"No." She shrank from him, stumbling several steps backwards. The lights of the truck stop seemed miles away. He met her retreat with forward strides of his own. He was too close.

Suddenly, Anna was back in the supply room at the agency. She'd dropped a box. The lid came off and sheets of paper scattered all over the floor. Liam stepped into the room moments later, his face turning red when he saw the mess.

She apologized and promised she'd clean it up. He said she'd better. He then grabbed her by the arm and pushed her against the wall, insisting that every last sheet of paper had better be usable when she was finished.

Anna felt fear creep up her spine and burrow itself in her chest.

She took another step away from the man in front of her. "Please, leave me alone."

His eyes widened and he held up his hands in surrender.

She didn't wait long enough to see what happened next. Turning towards her van, she took off at a run. She paid no attention to traffic. The sharp sound of a horn blasting barely made it through the fog.

At the van, Anna hit the side with more force than she'd intended. She unlocked the door, jumped inside, and locked it again.

Her heart pounded in her chest and she realized she was panting.

Calm down, Anna. Lord, help me calm down.

Epic whined and lifted himself until the front half of his body draped over her lap. His weight combined with the extra oxygen helped slow the adrenaline coursing through her body. She allowed herself to bury her face in Epic's fur. "Thanks, friend. You always know exactly what I need."

Tears pricked at her eyelids.

She shuddered against the memory that running into the guy in the parking lot had evoked. It was the first time Liam had put a hand on her when he became angry. Her confusion and shock still registered as though it'd just happened.

Even states away, Liam still had a real hold on her life.

The next morning, Anna held back a yawn. After the incident in the parking lot, she hadn't slept well most of the night. She'd also decided she wouldn't be going there for showers in the evenings anymore. Getting up earlier in the morning sounded like a much better alternative.

She tried to focus on slicing tomatoes before she added the tip of a finger to the bin.

The song on the radio ended and a commercial aired. Courtney cleared her throat. "How long have you been in Quintin?"

Anna guessed her co-worker to be around twenty-one. The only thing Courtney seemed to like to do more than talk was sing.

"I've been here a while." Anna cringed at the half truth. Well, compared to an afternoon, it had been a while. "It's a nice town. You?"

"I was born here. I'm going to college in Fort Worth now."

"What are you studying?"

Courtney moved her pile of onion slices to one of the food bins. "Business."

A song came on then and Courtney went back to singing. The less anyone here knew of her past, the better. Which was fine by Anna.

Courtney reminded Anna a little of Callie, a friend she'd made at the advertising agency. While Courtney was more of a free spirit, they both had an air of positivity that Anna found refreshing.

Thinking about her friend made her frown. Callie had been proof you never truly knew a person. When Anna shared how Liam reacted to the dropped paper, Callie told her maybe she overreacted and she should be grateful to have Liam for a boyfriend. Anna didn't confide in her friend again after that.

Anna finished with the tomatoes and moved on to the lettuce. There was no sense in dwelling on the past now. She had to take things one day at a time. One goal at a time.

"It's five minutes till ten!" Joel's deep voice carried to them from the front.

Without missing a beat, Courtney switched the radio off and kept singing along to the tune that must've continued to play in her head. She halted. "You going to the cookout?"

Anna's confusion must have been obvious because Courtney elaborated.

"Joel has all of us over to his house the first Sunday in March for a steak dinner. It's awesome. He does this almost every spring and fall break. Are you coming?"

Anna shrugged. "I hadn't heard about it. I'm not sure I'm invited."

Courtney raised her voice and shouted to the front, "Hey, boss! Anna's invited to the cookout, right?"

Joel appeared around the corner. "Of course. Wow, that's this Sunday, isn't it? I guess I'd better order some steaks." He gave them a wink. "I'll print out directions. I'll provide the meat and drinks. All you'll need to bring is your favorite side or dessert."

"That sounds like fun."

Joel left the room. The scent of his cologne, however, remained. Anna was beginning to associate the hints of pine and spice with him. Too bad he was her boss. The man was helpful, handsome, and he smelled good, too. A dangerous combination.

Anna forced her mind to a safer topic. The cookout. She had mixed feelings about the event. A big part of her looked forward to it. She couldn't remember the last time she'd had a steak.

But a social gathering would undoubtedly lead to questions. Questions she didn't want to field. The thought alone turned her stomach into knots.

She couldn't avoid other people forever, though. And eventually she'd be at home here in Quintin. That meant making new friends. Right? So far, the people she'd met at the diner had been nice enough.

Anna shivered. After everything with Liam and Callie, she wondered if she might be better off staying on her own. Someday, she'd own a large place and become the old cat lady — but with dogs instead.

She pictured a houseful of Epics and chuckled. No one in their right mind would step a toenail into her home.

Chapter Five

"Have you heard from Brooke?"

Chess's insistent voice brought Joel's attention to him. He paused the boxing game he was playing on the console and checked the clock. It was Thursday and a few minutes after ten in the evening. "Not a thing."

Chess grunted and leaned against the bar that separated the living room from the kitchen. He hooked his thumbs into the belt loops of his pants.

Joel stood from the couch and turned. "What's wrong?"

"She went on a dinner date with Paul. She has work first thing in the morning. I didn't expect her to be out this late."

Joel figured Brooke would be back by now, too. But it wasn't like this was the first time she'd stayed out late. Especially with her boyfriend. "This is the first date they've had in a couple of weeks. She works hard, Chess. She deserves to get out once in a while." Even so, concern had him anxious for her to return now.

Chess clenched his jaw but said nothing. He disappeared into the kitchen and returned a few minutes later with a bottle of soda. He sat down on a chair to watch Joel play his game but was up moments later pacing the room.

At eleven thirty, Joel turned the game off. He glanced over to find Chess glaring at the clock, his expression tight.

Joel thought back over the last couple of days, trying to discern why Chess would be this upset.

Relief flowed through Joel when the front door opened and Brooke walked through. She closed it behind her and turned to greet them. The tense half-smile on her face fell immediately when she noticed Chess. "Who died?"

"Do you have any idea what time it is?" Chess pushed away from the bar. "The least you could have done was text us and let us know you were going to be out late."

"Are you kidding me?" Brooke observed Chess, her mouth partway open. "I didn't think you'd want a play-by-play of my date."

Chess strode to stand in front of her, clearly not about to back down. "It's late, Brooke. Don't you have to be up for work at five in the morning? This is unlike you — to be out half the night."

Brooke's eyes flashed. "Back off, Chess."

Joel cringed at the exchange. The two tended to butt heads from time to time. But still, getting this upset at each other was rare.

Brooke shrugged off her jacket and threw it at Chess. "It's late and I'm tired. I'm going to bed." She offered Joel an apologetic look and went upstairs towards her bedroom.

Chess tossed the jacket onto the couch and moved to follow her.

Joel stepped forward. "Let me talk to her. I don't think …"

"…she's going to open the door for me. Yeah." Chess held back and Joel followed Brooke.

He took the stairs two at a time and finally knocked on the door to her room. "Brooke, it's Joel. May I come in?"

There was a moment of silence before her voice filtered through. "It's unlocked."

Joel found her sitting on the edge of her bed. She peered up at him, her eyes filled with tears while her fists clenched and unclenched in her lap. He joined her, sitting close enough to extend comfort but not quite touching her.

"Are you okay?"

"He makes me angry! I barely step inside and he confronts me like I'm a child."

Joel had seen it, too. Chess had been protective of all of them since they'd joined as a family. But it was especially true of Brooke. "He was worried about you."

"He's obsessed with being in control. I'm tired of it." Brooke let out a long breath. "Do you know where I was tonight?" When Joel shook his head, she continued. "I was supposed to meet Paul at the movie theater. He never showed. I spent all evening nursing a cookie and reading at the bookstore. Because I didn't want to come home and have you all feeling sorry for me. How pathetic is that?" She sniffed.

"That was messed up, Brooke. I'm sorry." Joel clenched his fist. You don't do that to a woman, much less one you've been dating for six months. It wouldn't do any good to express his thoughts to her now, though. "You deserve better. I hope you realize that."

"Would it have killed Chess to ask if I was okay first?" Her shoulders sagged, and a tear slipped down her cheek.

Joel put an arm around her and she rested her head against his shoulder. "Are you?"

She shrugged. "Paul's going to call it quits. Why else wouldn't he show up? I'll be fine — I've been through worse. I'm going to get some sleep."

He gave her a hug. "If you need anything, holler."

"I will." Brooke gave him a watery smile as he stood and moved towards the door. "Thanks, Joel."

He winked and left, closing the door behind him. It was a good thing he didn't run into Paul right now or the guy might be limping his way out of the house.

Joel withdrew his dad's folded knife from his pocket and found comfort from the weight of it in his hand.

Chess waiting for him in the living room. "Is she all right?"

"Yes. She's going to bed." Joel tossed the knife into the air and caught it. "She had a rough night. Paul stood her up and she didn't want to seem pathetic. She's been sitting at the bookstore all evening. She was already on edge when she came home." He didn't say he thought both Chess and Brooke had overreacted towards each other. He stamped down his frustration at the situation. "I'll let you go so you can get some rest." He waved his farewell and went to his own room.

As he readied for bed, memories of the many fights he'd witnessed in foster care came to the surface. He would turn up the music and pretend like he couldn't hear the damaging words fired back and forth. That particular placement lasted a long eight months. It'd been a relief when he'd moved. At the time, he didn't care where he was going.

Even now, he cringed when those closest to him yelled at each other like Chess and Brooke had... It was one of the few things Joel couldn't stand. He mentally pushed down the bile that had risen after the confrontation. "God, help Chess and Brooke smooth things over. And please protect Brooke's heart."

His eyes focused on his pocket knife sitting on the side table. The memories of watching his dad use it to transform a piece of wood into something intricate usually brought comfort. Even still, it took time before he could relax enough to fall asleep.

❧ ♥ ❧

The next day, Joel got off the phone with one of his suppliers. It was Friday and not one of the best days of the week to get a situation sorted out. The music Courtney was playing was loud enough that he'd had to take his paperwork and step outside. He didn't mind, though.

Courtney's singing floated to his ears the moment he stepped back in. That was nothing unusual. It was the second voice that joined hers which struck him right in the chest. Anastasia. Her normal speaking voice was quiet. The strength he heard while she sang surprised him. He let the notes wash over him until the song was over and a commercial break came on.

He'd only seen a handful of small smiles from Anastasia since she started working there. She had dimples in both of her cheeks. He'd caught little glimpses of them on occasion. But most of the time, she approached everything with quiet contemplation.

He hoped the fact she was singing with Courtney was a sign she was beginning to relax.

This was Anastasia's third day working at the diner and he'd noticed she never talked about herself. Which had him more curious about what brought her here. He had to admit he was looking forward to having his employees over Sunday. Maybe being in a more casual setting would help her open up a little.

He noticed the first day that she took her burger and fries and left the diner for the entire hour she had for lunch. Yesterday, he'd seen her maneuver her way across the parking lot to a van. She sat at a picnic table and ate, a large white dog at her feet. Interesting that she was bringing her dog with her. If she was staying at a hotel, she probably wasn't allowed to leave him in the room alone.

The sound of plastic clattering to the floor echoed through the building. Joel jogged around the corner to find Anastasia staring down at a sea of lettuce around her feet.

When she spotted him, she flinched. "I'm sorry. I should have dried my hands before trying to carry the bin and dropping it. I'll gladly pay you for the lettuce I've ruined."

Joel glanced from Anastasia to Courtney and back again. Was Anastasia scared of him? From the way she was breathing quickly and the wide eyes, he thought she might be. Losing a whole bin of lettuce wasn't great, but it could be much worse.

"It's just lettuce. Accidents happen."

Anastasia's hands shook. There was something else going on. Joel turned to Courtney, who seemed as surprised as he was. He pointed to the lettuce. "Will you dump that in the trash? I'll be right back."

She agreed.

Joel motioned to the front of the store. "May I speak with you a moment?" He waited until they'd reached the dining area. "Are you all right, Anastasia? You seem shaken."

"It's Anna." Her voice was scarcely above a whisper. Her face was pale. She stared through the window at the park beyond.

Joel didn't comment.

She reached for a section of her ponytail, wrapping the hair around a finger. To her credit, she raised her chin and met his eyes. Determination swirled with apprehension in their depths.

Joel had a sudden urge to pull her into his arms for a hug. Instead, he sat on the corner of a table in order make himself about the same height as she.

She crossed her arms over her chest defensively. She didn't speak and Joel took a deep breath. "It was an accident. They happen. If you think that's bad, I once dropped an entire stack of hamburger patties." He raised an eyebrow. "I don't expect you to pay for something you dropped. In the few days you've been here, you've proven to be one of my hardest working employees."

She digested that information and her shoulders sagged a little. Disbelief flashed across her face.

Joel watched her closely. *What just happened here?* Had someone been unkind to her in the past? The idea made him angry.

"Thank you." Her words were quiet. "I'll go prepare another bin of lettuce right away. I'll make sure I dry my hands this time."

She was watching him as though trying to figure something out. He half expected her to ask a question, but she turned and left the room.

Joel exhaled slowly. The vulnerability on her face when he'd walked in on the mess flashed in his mind. There was something about her that triggered his protective instincts. He may not know her well, but he'd seen enough to make it hard to imagine why anyone would want to hurt her.

The rest of the day went smoothly. Anastasia was a little more quiet all afternoon and left quickly when her shift was over at six. Joel watched her walk across the parking lot to her green van before returning his attention to the customers coming in the door.

At the end of the night, he finished closing up with the help of a manager. He was heading to his car when he identified Anastasia's van still sitting in the parking lot, barely illuminated by the streetlights.

Concern flared. Had something happened to her after she got off work?

His throat constricted as he jogged across the parking lot, praying everything was okay.

Chapter Six

Anna was using a flashlight to illuminate the book she was reading. She'd gone to the library in hopes of getting a card. But they insisted on seeing ID or a piece of mail showing her local address. Something she didn't have. Thankfully, a bookshelf in the lobby had paperbacks available to borrow, keep, or add to. She grabbed a few titles to help her pass away the evenings.

This particular novel was holding her interest a lot better here in the van at eight thirty in the evening than it probably would have otherwise.

A tapping sound on the driver's side window threw Anna's heart in her throat. She lurched upright as Epic filled the van with his deep barks.

Anna shined her flashlight through the window and lit up Joel's face. She pressed a fist to her chest in an attempt to calm the tremors that ran through her body. "What are you doing here?" she asked through the glass of the window.

Joel's eyebrows shot up. "I might ask you the same thing." He moved his head in an attempt to see around her. "Are you having car trouble?"

Epic stopped barking and whined softly, his log of a tail whacking the back of her chair.

"No, we're fine." It was probably too much to hope that he'd take her word for it and move on.

Joel cupped his hands around his face and peered into the second window down. When he came back, his face was filled with concern. "You're sleeping in your van?"

Anna groaned. There was no way to dig herself out of this one. Not at this point. She rolled the window down and then had to elbow Epic's head out of the way when he tried to step over her lap to welcome Joel.

"It's only temporary. But yes."

Joel opened his mouth as if to stay something and then closed it again. She saw the muscles in his jaw working. "How long have you been living this way?"

She considered trying to direct the conversation away from her situation. One glimpse of his eyes and it was clear that wouldn't work. "About a week. Give or take a couple of days."

If possible, his eyes widened even more. "You've been sleeping out here since you started working for me?"

Epic had moved to the next seat back and was trying to shove his head in the space between her seat and the side of the van to get to the open window.

"Oh good grief," Anna muttered. Why couldn't Joel see she was okay and not push the issue? She chucked her book onto the dash, unlocked the door, and clambered out. Epic followed her and the moment his giant paws touched the pavement, she pointed to him. "Sit."

Epic obeyed, his whole body quivering with his barely-contained need to greet their guest. That he had even calmed down surprised Anna.

Joel must have taken pity because he held a hand out to Epic and then proceeded to scratch his ears. The dog closed his eyes, his tongue hanging out, as he groaned with joy.

Anna blinked at her dog. Epic had hated Liam and wouldn't let the guy anywhere near him. Now here he was, practically falling all over himself to get Joel to pet him.

Anna made sure no one else was around and allowed Epic to wander in the grass nearby.

Joel shifted his weight and seemed willing to wait her out for more information.

"I'm fine. We're fine." She jerked a thumb in Epic's direction. "Do you think anyone's going to mess with me when I have him by my side?"

He tipped his head in acknowledgment of her point. "Still, this isn't a good idea."

"Good idea or not, I have no choice. And I'm saving up my paychecks to rent an apartment or something. Another three weeks at the most." Anna was getting a headache and didn't want to talk about it anymore. "Did you just close up the diner?"

"Yeah. I noticed your van. I was worried something had happened since it was still here over two hours after you got off work."

He was watching her closely and Anna was suddenly self-conscious. He was too observant. She hadn't realized he even knew which vehicle was hers. So much for staying at the edge of the lot near the park to keep from being noticed. "Your concern is appreciated. But I promise I'm fine."

He didn't look convinced. A breeze kicked up and Anna crossed her arms against it. She wished he'd go and let her get back inside where it was warmer.

Joel pulled his phone out and checked something on it. He frowned and shoved it back in his pocket again. "The temperature's supposed to get down to thirty-seven." He seemed thoughtful. "I'll get you a hotel room for tonight. We can figure something out tomorrow."

We? Was he serious? "Absolutely not. I'm not going to have you or anyone else pay for a hotel. They're not going to let my dog in anyway." She snapped her fingers when Epic wandered too far. He trotted back to her and sat by her side. "One paycheck, maybe two, and I'll be able to search for something else." She smiled, hoping to set him at ease. "Thank you, though. If you don't mind, I'm going to get back inside."

Oh, Joel minded. Maybe it wouldn't technically freeze tonight, but it was still way too cold for her to be sleeping out here in the parking lot. He knew firsthand how dangerous exposure to the weather could be.

He shoved memories aside and focused on the pretty woman in front of him. She was shivering.

"I'm not comfortable leaving you here like this."

Anastasia sighed and leaned against her vehicle. He had no doubt she was getting annoyed with him.

Her dog went to stand next to her. His shoulder came up to Anastasia's chest.

Joel blinked at them. "No wonder you own a van."

Anastasia reached over to rub the dog's ear. "I know. He's a monster." She barely had to bend down to hook an arm under the dog's chin and rest her cheek against his head.

"What's his name?"

"Epic."

Joel laughed loudly. "Fitting. He seems friendly."

Epic moved to lick his hand. Anastasia grunted. "Apparently he is to you."

What did she mean by that? He straightened and pointed behind him. "Will you please come with me to the diner where we can talk? It's warmer." No reply. "Anastasia?"

She rolled her eyes. "It's Anna. And get in. I'll drive us over."

Before she changed her mind, Joel jogged around the van and opened the passenger door. Anastasia was ushering Epic inside and the dog promptly planted himself on the seat in front of Joel.

She grinned, a dimple appearing in each cheek. "You'll have to sit in the back. That's Epic's spot."

Joel might have thought she was kidding except for the way Epic kept his eyes straight ahead as though waiting to be driven by the chauffeur. Joel chuckled and did as she'd suggested.

He pointed at the steering wheel. "Can you see over that to drive?"

Anastasia lifted herself up to her full height. "Are you taking a jab at my short stature now?" She jerked a thumb at him. "This coming from the giant who may or may not be able to get out of my van without hitting his head."

Joel tipped his head back and laughed loudly. "Touché."

They drove across the parking lot. Joel unlocked the front door of the diner and turned the interior lights on again. After being outside, the warmth felt wonderful. He waved to one of the corner booths. "Have a seat. I'll be right back."

He returned with sodas: A root beer for himself and a cola for Anastasia. She took a swig from the straw. "Thank you. How'd you know I like cola?"

Joel shrugged. He'd caught himself watching her multiple times since he'd met her. He had no intention of going out with her like Brooke suggested. But he'd have to be dead to not admire her beauty or her spunk. "It's what you get to go with your lunch, isn't it?"

He slid into the horseshoe shaped booth and sat almost across from her. He had two of these booths in his diner. They reminded him of something he'd have seen in the fifties with red cushions and backings. He'd completed the theme with silver accents. More than just a business, the diner was also his hobby.

"Well, thank you."

"You're welcome." He rested his arms on the tabletop, the surface smooth and cold. His mind flew to the falling temperatures outside. "Listen, I know I have no right to push this. But I can't, in good conscience, leave you sleeping in your van."

Anastasia leaned forward and raked the fingers of both hands through her hair. "You're very kind and I don't want you to think I don't appreciate it.

But I've got this under control. I don't need anyone's pity."

"There's a difference between pity and worry."

"And I'm not yours to worry about." The awkward phrasing brought heat to her cheeks. "You know what I mean."

He let out a deep chuckle. "Yes, I do." He suddenly wondered if her hair was as silky as it appeared.

Wait, what?

He pulled his thoughts back on track. The truth was, he'd react this way if he found any of his employees sleeping in their vehicle. Her soft hair and vulnerable eyes had nothing to do with it.

Brooke would call him a liar right now. But Joel knew his friends wouldn't want Anastasia in her current circumstance, either.

No matter how much he hated this, there wasn't much he could do about her situation tonight. Especially if she was unwilling to let him.

Anastasia cleared her throat. As if reading his mind, she said, "I warm the van right before Epic and I go to sleep. Between that, a slew of blankets, and Epic's furnace-like body, we're fine overnight."

They sat silently, watching each other. An invisible thread of electricity traveled between them. Joel had no idea what to do with it, either. Did she feel it as well, or was he imagining the whole thing?

Joel cleared his throat and absently moved his cup from one spot on the table to another. Anything to keep from acting on his instincts to reach over and take Anastasia's hand in his.

He walked to the back and got a piece of paper and a pen. When he returned, he wrote his cell number down. "If you need anything, please promise to call me."

She left the paper lying on the table. "We'll be fine. We've got our routine. Showers at the truck stop, this park during the weekdays. Maybe tour other parks on the weekends." She almost seemed surprised that she'd shared this much. She tipped her head and let it rest against the back of her seat. "I had hoped to get through the next month without anyone finding out."

Joel let that go without a comment. "Would you like to join me for breakfast tomorrow?"

"Epic and I have it covered. Thank you, though."

"Oh? What are you planning on eating?" He hiked an eyebrow at her.

"Are you for real?" Anastasia stared at him.

"I'm serious. What do you eat for breakfast?"

"I have a box of cereal with my name on it." She motioned behind her. "I've even got orange juice to go with it."

Something dawned on him. "No wonder you pushed for having a burger included in the job I gave you." He should have figured there was more to it than trying to eek something extra from the position. "And dinner?"

"I have sandwich fixings."

He had to admit it was pretty impressive. She'd thought of everything. Epic seemed well cared for and Joel was certain she had a great watchdog on her hands. She hadn't been late to work yet and she did a fantastic job. He had nothing to complain about there.

But the fact still remained. He couldn't force Anastasia to leave her van. He couldn't make her call him if she needed help.

But he would find an alternative place for her to live.

They finished their sodas and Joel escorted her back out of the diner. "Will you do me a favor?"

Anastasia turned. "What's that?"

"Will you stay parked here near the diner tonight? It's lighter." Yeah, it sounded lame to his ears, too.

Her lips twitched in amusement but she acquiesced with a bob of her head. She opened the van door and Epic immediately stuck his head out, his body moving back and forth from the power of his wagging tail.

Joel reached a hand out to pat the monster dog's head. His eyes, however, were on Anastasia. "Stay safe, huh? I'll see you tomorrow?"

"Tomorrow."

He'd grabbed the paper with his number off the table on the way out. He reached out and took her hand in his, placing the paper against her palm. "Just in case."

"Thank you." She gave him a small smile and climbed inside.

Joel made sure the door was locked and shut it behind her. With a final wave, he turned and made his way back to his car, going against every instinct screaming to do the opposite.

What had happened in her past that she'd be living in her vehicle right now? He'd like to think she was going overboard to save money like she said, but something told him it was more than that.

Anastasia was one mystery after another.

Chapter Seven

After Joel drove away, Anna smoothed out the paper containing his contact information. She had no intention of using it, though. She put his name and phone number in the contacts list on her phone.

She ought to be annoyed that he not only stuck his nose in her business, but thought he had a right to suggest she change her situation. It shouldn't matter to him where she sleeps as long as she gets to work on time.

Then why wasn't she angry with him? Wasn't that exactly what Liam did — try to dictate her life?

No. This was different.

Liam wanted to know where she went and what she was doing when he wasn't with her. He wanted to make sure that she waited for him or, in the case of work, fetched something for him.

Joel... He was concerned for *her*. She couldn't think of a thing he'd gotten out of trying to help her. Before this, when was the last time someone had shown a genuine concern for her?

Not since Grandma and Grandpa passed.

The thought brought moisture to her eyes.

It'd been long enough that she forgot people actually did that for each other.

Once she and Liam had become a couple, it'd taken a while for her to understand how controlling he truly was. They'd been together for six months when Anna knew she had to get out before things got worse.

Anna was walking to her car after working late. She was about to slide into the driver's seat when Liam called her name. His face red, he pointed a thick finger at Anna and roared. "You did it!"

Anna had no idea what he was talking about. She shrank from his glare and waited for him to explain himself.

"We were short three hundred dollars after closing yesterday. Someone took that money before it was placed in the safe. You're not going to get away with it."

Shaking her head, Anna tried to form the words to defend herself. She hadn't taken the money – never would have thought of it.

She considered the idea that he was making it up. He was furious. When he got like this, she tried to lie low. Become invisible. But this time, his anger was directed towards her. Panic made her heart pound. "I didn't take it, Liam. Not a cent."

"Someone did. And if you don't come up with the missing money, I'm going to find a way to prove you took it."

Anna had no idea what to do. She'd been saving what money she could. Most of what he paid her went towards her tiny apartment. Ever since he'd hurt her arm in the supply room, she'd been planning a way to move and start over. But she'd need her money to do that — she couldn't afford to give him any of it.

She took a step towards her car, but Liam blocked her path. "Where do you think you're going?"

"Home, Liam. I didn't take your money and I don't have any to give you, either. Please, let me go."

He sneered and latched onto her wrist. "You're not going anywhere." His eyes narrowed. "You come back inside with me or you can kiss your job goodbye."

Anna jerked her arm away, her wrist throbbing. Courage bubbled up from inside. "Then consider this my resignation. I'm done. We're done."

He cursed and sputtered. "You can't walk away from me. I made you. You're never going to make it on your own, Anna. Not without me. You're nothing without me."

She managed to get into her car and lock the door before he stopped her. He kicked her car with enough force to create vibrations that traveled up Anna's spine.

"This isn't the end. I'll make life difficult for you."

Anna flexed her wrist. The pain had disappeared, but the memories remained vivid as ever.

She readied for bed and lay on the bench seat, blankets piled high.

How had she trusted him in the first place? She wanted to blame herself. But the truth was, he was a con man. And a good one at that. He'd duped her from the beginning.

And there was a very real possibility that he was searching for her right now. She shivered.

If Joel noticed her van and wondered why she was there in the parking lot, staying in one place would make it easier for Liam to spot her, too. Maybe she needed to rotate between parks. Try to stay on the move until she rented an apartment. Once she did, she'd ditch the van and take the bus to and from work if she had to. Whatever it took to stay off Liam's radar.

Her hand brushed against the container on Epic's collar that held the thumb drive. She didn't work on Monday. She would find someone to help her open those files. There had to be evidence showing exactly what Liam had been up to.

Because he wasn't going to give up searching for her if she didn't find a way to get him behind bars.

Her thoughts shifted to Joel. Even in the beginning with Liam, he'd never shown her the kindness or respect that Joel had in the few days she'd known him.

She focused on Joel as she closed her eyes, falling asleep faster than she had in days.

❧ ♥ ❧

Anna woke the next morning and drove to the truck stop for a shower. Later, she claimed a spot near the park and gave Epic the chance to exercise for a bit. It was chilly, but he didn't seem to care.

There was still an hour before work began. She settled on the picnic table bench.

Moments later, Epic barked and stared behind her.

Anna jumped to her feet and whirled around, heart pounding in her chest. It was Joel, but still. That he'd gotten as close as her van before she noticed him showed she wasn't paying enough attention.

Epic bounded towards Joel but she snapped her fingers. "No, Epic. Sit."

Joel set a drink holder down with four insulated cups in it on the picnic table. "Good morning."

"Good morning." Her eyes went from the drinks to him again. "What's going on?"

"I thought you could use something warm to drink this morning, but I didn't know what you liked." His expression was open and his dark eyes hopeful. "I brought coffee, hot green tea, and hot chocolate."

"What's in the fourth cup?"

"Another coffee." Joel put a hand in his coat pocket and pulled out a sizable collection of packets containing sugar and creamer. "I don't do mornings without it. Take your pick."

Anna watched as he withdrew a cup and added two sugars, gave the coffee a stir, and replaced the lid. He sat down at the table without a thought.

Her eyebrows rose. That was incredibly presumptuous.

But it was cold. She chose the hot chocolate. "Thank you."

"You're welcome."

When Epic wagged his tail, his entire body wriggled in response. Anna shook her head. "He wants to come say hello to you. He sure likes you."

Joel held a hand out and that's all the invitation Epic needed. After that, Joel was hard pressed to keep the giant from climbing into his lap. "I'm glad. I don't think his owner has made up her mind yet, though."

Heat flooded to Anna's cheeks. He must have

noticed because she caught a grin on his face before he turned back to the dog.

Not for the first time, Anna considered the idea that Joel was one of those genuinely nice guys she'd heard so much about. A gentleman like her grandfather had been. She studied his profile, admiring his strong chin and long eyelashes. Most women would kill for those gorgeous lashes.

His eyes found hers and she blushed to the roots of her hair. She jumped up and went to the van to check her phone as an excuse to hide her face.

"What brings you out here so early this morning?" He was silent and when she turned around, he looked uncertain. Epic had gone back to wandering in the grass nearby. Joel took a drink of his coffee. Anna sat down again, this time across the table from him.

Joel focused on her. "You don't have any family, do you, Anastasia?"

"Why do you always call me Anastasia? Most people I've known are relieved I go by Anna because my full name is too unusual."

"That surprises me. I'd like to continue calling you Anastasia if you'd let me. It's an elegant name. It suits you."

The breeze shifted, and she caught a whiff of his cologne. Anna dipped her head slightly, giving him permission. She'd never thought her name pretty, but now… It seemed special. Which was insane.

"You never did answer my question about whether or not you have any family."

Anna rested her arms on the picnic table. She didn't want to talk about it. But there was something in Joel's expression that told her he understood.

He took a deep breath. "I live in a house with two other people. I don't have any biological family, but Chess and Brooke might as well be." He fiddled with the drink holder. "We all spent a fair amount of time in the foster care system. I guess we decided to create our own family. Chess says we reinvented family — made it better."

Anna turned her head to peek at him from beneath her eyelashes. "It sounds like a real blessing you all ended up together." Her voice sounded wistful even to her own ears. "I don't have family, either. Not since I lost my grandparents. How did you know?"

Joel seemed to mull over his response. "Maybe those of us who have had to grow up alone are able to recognize each other."

Joel watched Anastasia as she absorbed what he'd just said. Her head bobbed slightly, her eyes fixed on the ground.

It was interesting how she seemed tough — self-assured — one minute, and then vulnerable the next. The thought of her sleeping in her van still made him uneasy. "You're welcome to park up by the diner at night from now on."

She shot him a sideways glance. "Actually, I may start rotating parks. Change up the routine. If you noticed us, others might as well. I don't want to get in trouble. It's not legal to camp out in most public places like I've been."

He hadn't considered the fact that she might not stay in the store's parking lot. Of all the parks in town, this was probably one of the safer ones. And it made him feel better knowing she wasn't far from the diner, too.

Without thinking it through, he blurted out, "You're welcome to come and stay at my house. Our house. Brooke's there. It's not like you're coming to live with a bunch of guys. We have plenty of room for you."

Nope, that was not one of the more intelligent things he'd ever said.

Anastasia bristled, her spine straightening. She stood and brushed off the back of her pants. "I'm not a charity case. I'm not your responsibility. And I thank you for not dragging your family into my business, too."

Joel jumped to his feet and reached for her arm to stop her from rushing away. "Anastasia, wait. I'm sorry."

She moved away from him, his hand dropping back to his side. "You should go on to work. I have a few things to tie up here and then I'll be there shortly. It's almost nine." With that, she called Epic and marched towards her van.

Joel groaned. *Stupid!* Whatever ground he'd gained yesterday and today had been lost in a matter of minutes.

If the way her pretty lips were pinched together were any indication, he'd be lucky if she spoke to him again today.

Chapter Eight

Who did Joel think he was, anyway? Anna had fumed about his annoying offer all day. He'd tossed an apologetic glance her way several times at work and she'd taken her leave immediately after her shift ended.

The last thing she needed was for Joel to insist she change the way she was managing her life. She'd had more than enough of that with Liam.

What was it with her and bosses?

Except there was a difference between trying to control her life, and being overly concerned.

It was still none of his business. And she certainly wasn't going to go and sleep on a couch in some stranger's house.

She half expected him to come by the van and check on her after he closed the diner. He hadn't though. Anna was mostly relieved. It was the tiny twinge of disappointment that bothered her the most.

Anna decided to stay in this park, although she did move the large van closer to the diner after Joel left.

She'd considered rotating locations. But assuming Liam was willing to chase her this far, locating her would be a matter of luck. It was probably best to stay put. She had to hope he'd either given up, or she'd made it hard enough to track her and she could get into an apartment before he ever reached Quintin.

Liam reached for his cell phone the moment it rang. When he saw Rick's name on the caller ID, he punched the screen to answer. "Did you find her, yet?"

He pictured the tiny man's face turning red. Rick never did like being pushed. But it paid to have a contact who was a private detective — especially when the man owed him a favor.

After getting the license plate number of the green van Anna had purchased, he called Rick up and fed him the information.

It'd been several days. He needed answers.

The sound of Rick clearing his throat came over the line. "I finally got a hit on that license plate number. It turned up in Dallas, Texas. She drove on a highway that charges a toll and her plate was photographed."

Liam stood up, his boots hitting the floor with a clunk. "Which highway? When?"

He jotted the information down on a piece of paper while Rick talked. Anna had traveled further than he thought she'd have the guts to go.

Rick's voice interrupted Liam's thoughts. "Can I

assume my debt to you has been paid?"

Liam barked into the phone. "Not even close. Keep searching. She could go anywhere from Dallas. I want to know where she is now." He hung up and tossed the phone onto the counter.

He decided it'd be worth it to head towards Texas. If Rick valued his job as a private detective, he'd get more information. Possibly before Liam even reached Dallas.

Anna couldn't keep this pace up forever. At some point, she was going to stop somewhere. And when she did...

"Don't worry, honey, I'm going to find you." He grinned. She'd either return willingly to Utah with him, or he'd make sure she'd never run again.

❦

Joel had hoped seeing the location for a potential second diner would've helped the decision-making process. He had to admit it had great visibility in a high-traffic part of town. But the thought of fighting that same traffic on a workday made his stomach churn.

He groaned as a chime sounded, announcing he'd received a text. He pulled his phone out of his back pocket and glanced at the message from Chess.

Brooke's boyfriend came by and it didn't go well. She's upset.

Joel texted back.

I'm coming home. Leaving Dallas now.

His chest tightened. At least it was Saturday and he wouldn't have to deal with rush hour traffic.

It was no secret that he was more able to reach Brooke than Chess could, but things must be bad if he'd been called home.

By the time he stepped into the house, Chess was pacing the living room with a bottle of soda in one hand.

As soon as Chess noticed Joel, he pointed a finger at him. "You need to go see if she's okay. She doesn't want to talk about it. She's been crying since the jerk left."

"What exactly happened?" Joel looked around the living room, noting that everything seemed to be in order.

Chess cleared his throat. "Paul came to the house today. Admitted he'd been cheating on Brooke and that's why he hadn't been around. But that he'd changed his mind, now, and wanted her back. Obviously, Brooke was devastated. She announced it was over, but he kept insisting she give him another chance."

Joel had a feeling this was only the beginning.

Chess stopped pacing. "She told him to leave. That's when he called her a worthless—" He finished the expletive, his nostrils flaring. "So I gave him a good punch to that pretty face of his and escorted him out of the house. I told him not to come back or he'd regret it." He patted the spot on his waist where his concealed handgun was located. "It's a good thing that did the trick."

Joel had been tempted to get his concealed handgun license as well but hadn't found the time.

Situations liked these always made him wish he made the effort.

Truthfully, Chess hadn't done anything Joel wouldn't have himself if he'd been there. His heart hurt for Brooke. He imagined how upset she was right now.

With an air of frustration, Chess collapsed onto the couch. "She's probably mad I hit the guy. But I'd do it again in a heartbeat." He stood up again to pace the room.

"I'll go talk to her." Moments later, Joel knocked on the door to her room. "May I come in?"

He twisted the doorknob and went through to find Brooke curled up on her bed. She wasn't crying, but her eyes were puffy and red.

"I heard what happened. I'm sorry, Brooke. You deserve much better than Paul."

"I'm not sorry he's gone. There's no way I'd be able to trust him again." She took in a shaky breath.

"Are you mad at Chess? You know he's taken responsibility for both of us — whether he should or not — since day one. He heard Paul disrespecting you and saw red. He acted on instinct. I can't promise I wouldn't have done the same thing."

Brooke sat up. "No. I wish I could've punched him myself." She shrugged. "I'm mad at myself, I guess. I knew there was something going on, but I still kept hoping ... And now I look like an idiot."

Joel sat down on the bed beside her. "No, you don't." He put an arm around her shoulders. "You're loyal and trusting. Don't sell yourself short. It's not your fault guys like Paul will take advantage of that. It's not a deficit in you — it shows just how messed up he is."

Brooke didn't look convinced. "I'm stuck in a rut, Joel. I need a change. I've been leaning that direction before all this happened. But now... I think it'd be good for me."

Her words settled in his stomach like a boulder. "What kind of change are you talking about?"

She kept her eyes on her hands. "I'm thinking about moving out. Getting a place of my own. It's about time, don't you agree?" When he didn't respond right away, she frowned. "Does that make me a horrible person?"

Joel's first instinct in any situation was to fix it. Find a way to piece things together in order to keep his family and friends safe and happy. His mind was running through different options that would give Brooke the change she needed without her needing to move out. But the dull look in her eyes and the trembling of her chin stopped him. "No, you're not a horrible person. You've always enjoyed a good adventure. You've got to do what's best for you." She started to talk but he held up a hand to stop her. "Take some time to think about it and pray. Make sure you're not jumping into a decision like this just because of Paul."

Brooke elbowed him, her eyes swimming with tears. "Thanks, Joel." She tipped her head back and rolled it to stretch her neck muscles. She sighed and let herself fall back onto the bed.

"For the record, I'll sure hate for you to leave. We're a family."

"I know." She frowned. "But even if I move out, I'll be here for you guys. It's not going to be all that different."

Joel doubted that last statement. Thinking about

their family breaking apart filled his gut with dread. But even in a conventional family, things had to change. "You going to be okay? I can cancel the barbecue tomorrow. My gang won't mind."

"No, I wouldn't dream of it. It'll be a good distraction. And I'll be fine. Eventually. I'm going to get out my chocolate stash and search the apartment listings. Or for a hit man for Paul. Only kidding. Mostly."

He stood and smiled at her. "Let me know if you need to talk. And Brooke?"

"Yeah?"

"Don't doubt yourself. You deserve a good guy and he's out there looking for you right now."

"I know. Thanks, Joel."

He smiled again before going back out to the living room. Chess was waiting when he entered.

"Brooke's going to be okay. She's too tough to let Paul get her down for long."

"Is she upset with me?"

"No. I think she's glad you popped him one." Joel wished he could've seen it.

Chess looked relieved. "Good. I half hope he comes back so I can give him another." His eyes narrowed. "Why do I get the feeling there's something else going on?"

As much as Joel dreaded the idea of Brooke moving out, he knew Chess would hate it even more. "She wants a change. Feels like she's stuck in a rut. We may need to prepare ourselves for the possibility that she'll move into a place of her own."

Chess shoved his fingers through his hair, his brow wrinkled.

Joel put a hand in his pocket and closed his fist

around his knife. He'd left Anastasia to sleep in the parking lot of his diner, Brooke was upstairs upset, and Chess was likely stressing about their family unit breaking apart.

When it came to wanting to fix things tonight, Joel had definitely struck out.

Chapter Nine

Anna woke slowly Sunday morning and tried not to disturb her furry partner. The temperature was frigid. Puffs of fog floated through the air with each breath. She pulled the comforter up to her nose and closed her eyes again. This was the first morning since she'd arrived in Texas that she second-guessed staying in her van.

But she didn't regret turning down Joel's offer to stay in his house last night. Not even now when her fingers felt frozen and the last thing she wanted to do was climb out from under the comforter.

The sounds of birds chattering in the trees filled the air, overriding the noise from the street filtering into the van.

She snuck a quick peek at her phone and was surprised it was after eight.

Epic heard her movements and was instantly on his feet. He shook, the van rocking slightly with the motion. He proceeded to nudge her arm with his cold nose.

"Did you sleep well, boy?" She scratched behind his ears. He closed his eyes in bliss and leaned his head to one side, causing Anna to chuckle. "Me, too." It was one of the few nights in the last week that she hadn't had a nightmare involving Liam or anything else that had happened at the advertising agency. She considered that a good sign.

If only she didn't have to go to the cookout. While the sky was clear, it was cold and windy. Joel had said the barbecue would take place, rain or shine. There was no way weather was going to get her out of the obligation.

The temptation to skip it would've won out if Anna hadn't told Courtney she'd be there. If she failed to show, no doubt her co-worker would have a dozen questions for her come Tuesday morning.

Anna forced herself to get up and turn on the van for warmth. Later, she took time to wash her clothes at the laundromat followed by a shower at the truck stop.

Thirty minutes before the cookout, she ran into the store and picked up sweet rolls and a tub of coleslaw. Hopefully that would be enough. If she'd been living anywhere else, she would have brought a handmade dessert. Grandma had always made something from scratch for an event like this.

She had to fight to keep from snatching one of the rolls and eating it on the way to the address Joel had provided for her. She wanted to make sure there were enough for everyone.

By the time she got there and found a spot to park on the street, she doubted the air had warmed more than five degrees since she first woke up. At least she wouldn't have to worry about Epic getting too warm in the van today. She patted him. "Be good and I'll try to save some leftovers for you."

Epic opened his mouth wide in what resembled a smile. Anna zipped up her windbreaker and grabbed the plastic bag of food in one hand. "Wish me luck."

The front door swung open before she reached it and a woman ushered her inside with the wave of an arm.

"Here, let me take that for you." The woman held onto the windbreaker as Anna shrugged it off. "My name's Brooke."

"Hi. I'm Anna." She wondered whether Joel had shared about her living situation with the rest of the family. She hoped not.

Brooke gave her a friendly smile. "Well, it's nice to meet you. If Joel and his diner haven't scared you away yet, that says something." She winked. "Follow me to the kitchen. Everyone's gathering in there or out under the covered back patio."

Anna took in the large house and its modest decor as she followed Brooke. She was relieved to spot Courtney and Adam, along with several other people from the diner, in the kitchen. At least it wasn't like she was the only one who wasn't part of the family here. They all welcomed her and Brooke took the bag of food from her to add to the bar that separated the kitchen from the living room.

"Isn't this weather insane?" Courtney wrinkled her nose. "Last year, it was beautiful. We played volleyball in the backyard."

Adam frowned. "Wind makes it hard to do much of anything outside."

Courtney took her by the arm. "Come on, let's go see how Joel's managing to keep the fire going." She led her to the back porch where Joel and some other men were standing around a barbecue pit.

Joel glanced up with a strained smile, concern skimming across his face. "I'm glad you could make it. This is my friend and roommate, Chess. Did you meet Brooke inside?"

Anna said she had. She was pretty sure nearly everyone who worked at the diner was here and they didn't need introductions. She liked that about the place — it was small and friendly. People knew each other and, if this was any indication, enjoyed getting together outside of work.

They would also be a good buffer between herself and a certain boss.

Joel lifted the lid of the grill and smoke billowed out. Riding along with the smoke were the intense scents of beef, garlic, and butter. Anna's stomach growled on cue.

Conversation floated around her as the others relayed a story from last year's spring break antics.

Chess stood next to her and jutted his chin towards Joel. "How do you like working at the diner?"

Anna studied him, uncertain. He wasn't nearly as tall as Joel, but he had a commanding presence. He was watching her, waiting for a response. "It's a challenge, but it's fun. The food is passable, even if my supervisor's a little bossy."

Chess laughter rumbled from his chest. "That sounds like Joel. You know, when he first told us he wanted to own and run a diner, I had my doubts. He's certainly made a success out of it."

Chess seemed proud of Joel. Anna had to admit she was glad she'd chosen to ask for a job at the diner. Even after having issues with Joel wanting to fix her living situation, it was a great place to work. She went through a mental list of questions she could ask Chess without personal ones coming back to her. Inquiring about his profession seemed safe. "What do you do for a living?"

"I'm a software engineer. I work for a place in Dallas, though I get to work from home several days a week. That helps with the long commute."

Interesting. Her mind jumped to the thumb drive. "Do you mind if I ask you a computer-related question?"

"Not at all."

"I have a file on a drive that I need to open. But it's encrypted. I don't suppose there's any way to open it, is there?"

Chess appeared thoughtful. "There might be. It depends on what type of encryption. I'll be happy to take a look for you if you'd like."

"Sure, that'd be great."

Joel announced that the steaks were done and everyone should move indoors. Anna planned to retrieve the drive sometime after they ate.

The meal was incredible. Anna ate her fill and then some, going back for seconds on the slaw. Conversation flowed easily and she relaxed. It was interesting to watch Joel interact with everyone outside of the diner. It turned out he and Brooke could tell funny stories. More than once, she ended up laughing until her eyes watered.

She couldn't remember the last time she'd laughed this much.

She had every intention of remaining mad at Joel. But it wasn't quite as easy when he kept working so hard to make people laugh. Especially when he turned that smile her direction, the crinkles around his eyes deepening. It wasn't fair for him to look that attractive.

Anna cleared her throat and turned to answer a question Courtney had asked her. The distraction was more than welcome.

An hour later, nearly all the guests departed. Anna would have left by then if it hadn't been for the conversation she'd been having with Courtney and Brooke. Now Courtney said she needed to leave to finish a paper due the next day and Anna found herself with Adam and the three members of the household.

Joel held up a hand. "You're both welcome to stay. We're going to watch one of the new Star Wars movies if you're interested."

Adam readily agreed. Anna would have bowed out even if Courtney were still there. The need to escape crawled across her skin. "I shouldn't. I appreciate the offer, though."

Brooke moved to stand next to her. "It'd be nice to not be the only female in the house." She grinned.

Anna searched for an excuse. "I'm not sure I can. My dog's waiting for me out in my van. I need to get us back and let him run around for a while."

Joel spoke up from his spot on the couch. "Bring him through the side gate into the backyard. He'll get some exercise. There's leftover steak he's welcome to. If you don't think he'll jump over the fence, he's welcome to stay out there until you leave."

Anna bit back a sigh. Yeah, she should've taken off when the first round of people left the gathering.

Brooke was watching her.

It would be nice to have something to do besides sit in the van all day. And it didn't look like she was going to get out of staying without a fight, anyway.

"If you're sure."

Joel held the gate open and Epic pranced right through, followed closely by his owner. Mesmerized by the way the wind tossed Anastasia's hair about her face, Joel cleared his throat and forced his gaze onto the mammoth dog before him. He held a hand out for Epic to smell and, moments later, lick. Joel looked from the dog to the fence. "Is he a jumper?"

"Truthfully, I have no idea. I guess we'll find out." She sounded nervous. Her gaze flitted to the gate behind her like she wished she could change her mind.

He understood. He'd been nervous all evening, wondering if she'd even come to the cookout, much less whether she'd be upset with him. She didn't seem to be angry, but then, they hadn't spoken privately until now, either.

"Tell you what. Why don't we let him loose and stay out here for a few minutes to see how he does?"

She nodded her agreement. The moment she removed the leash from Epic's collar, he went exploring.

Joel bent to retrieve a stick from the grass. He withdrew his pocket knife before taking a seat in one of the patio chairs that was partially protected from the wind. He motioned to another and Anastasia joined him. After opening his knife with one hand, he whittled away the bark on the stick.

She was silent as she watched Epic. The dog took interest in the curls of wood landing on the concrete by their feet.

Joel had enjoyed seeing Anastasia relax as the afternoon progressed. At one point, Joel caught her laughing and found himself completely captivated. It wasn't simply the sound of her laugh, but the way her dimples had come to life when she smiled. Truly smiled.

He took a quick peek at her profile from the corner of his eye. Not knowing how she felt about him now was worse than what she might say if he shined a light on the elephant in the room.

"I'm truly sorry about last night. It was never my intention to offend you or insinuate that you couldn't take care of yourself." He held a hand out. "Truce? I can't promise I won't worry about you out there — and I may even drop by to check on you from time to time — but I will do my best not to say anything else stupid."

She peered at his hand and then his face. Her own was deadpan and Joel worried until one corner of her mouth lifted. She shook her head. "I suppose. Let's keep that dropping by to a minimum, huh?"

Anastasia reached for his hand and his own engulfed it. The touch of her skin against his sent warmth straight to his heart. He didn't want to let it go. He did, though. And his hand felt cold without hers.

They sat in companionable silence for a few moments before she spoke again. "Everyone here seems great. You're lucky to have each other."

"Yes, we are. God answered prayers when he brought the three of us together. Don't ever lose the belief that he's got something in mind for you, too." When they'd both grown silent again, he decided to steer the conversation in another direction. "What are you going to do on your day off tomorrow?"

"I hate to spend the money, but I think I'm going to take Epic by the groomers and have his hair cut super short. The shedding is driving me crazy." She shrugged. "Other than that, I have no idea. How about you?"

"Our lawn needs to be mowed. I'm sure Brooke will have a list of things she'll want to get accomplished, too."

The sliding glass door opened and Chess stepped out. "If you have that drive, Anna, I'd be happy to take a look at the files for you before we begin the movie."

"Oh! Thank you! Give me a moment and I'll be inside."

Chess smiled and disappeared from sight.

Anastasia called Epic over and removed a metal cylinder from his collar.

Interesting.

Joel watched her and raised an eyebrow. She either didn't see or chose to ignore it.

He pocketed his knife and followed Anastasia inside moments later, wondering why she had some kind of thumb drive attached to Epic's collar. Chess had led her to his room that doubled as an office and was plugging the tiny drive into a USB slot.

"Let's see what we've got here."

A window opened up showing them a dozen

files, all with names that made no sense.

Chess turned to Anastasia. "Do you know which file you're after?"

She wound a section of hair around one finger. "I have no idea. I was hoping to go through them, but every time I click on one…"

Chess clicked on the first one and got an encryption message. Joel stepped close enough to read exactly what it said.

After trying several things to open the file, Chess finally closed the window. "I wish I could help. But these files are heavily encrypted. They require a two-factor passkey. It's a digital keychain that cycles through numerical passwords. You've got to have that to get the right password and view the files." He pulled the thumb drive out and handed it back to Anastasia. "I'm sorry."

"It's all right. I appreciate you trying." Her shoulders slumped as she clutched the drive in her hand and chewed on her lower lip. She left the room.

It wasn't until Joel heard her go outside again that he spoke with Chess. "Any idea what the files were?"

Chess grunted. "Most looked like spreadsheets. One was a database. I have no idea what they were for or what they contained, though."

Joel clapped him on the shoulder. "Thanks."

Anastasia was leaning against the doorframe. She didn't seem to have the thumb drive anymore and he assumed she put it back in the cylinder on Epic's collar. Joel stopped a few feet from her. "Are you okay?"

"Sure. I'm fine."

Yeah, he didn't believe that for one minute. "Any

chance you want to talk about the files?" He was pretty sure he already knew the answer to that.

"I can't." She released a heavy sigh. "We'd better get in there before they start the movie without us." She forced a laugh, but it never reached her eyes.

Joel followed her in and closed the door behind them. He sure wished he knew what was going on with her.

Chapter Ten

Anna stayed awake half the night trying to decide what to do. Since leaving Utah, she'd held out hope that someone would be able to open the files on that blasted thumb drive.

Now what was she going to do? Without the evidence she hoped the drive contained, she had no way to convince the police — or anyone else — of what Liam had done.

Maybe she could take the drive to the police. What were the odds they could decrypt the files if Chess wasn't able to?

What if they asked her where she got it? Figured out she stole it?

No. She was on her own for now.

She'd always assumed Liam would chase her down for the files on the drive. But if she couldn't have access to them because he still held the passkey, maybe he wasn't chasing her after all. What if he let her go, knowing it would be more effort than it was worth to hunt her down?

As much as she wanted to believe that was a possibility, she couldn't bank her safety on it.

Once she finally fell asleep, she had another dream about the fire. Only this time, instead of standing there laughing at her from the other side of the flames, Liam reached through, grabbed her arm, and dragged her right into them.

She awoke with a scream. The sky was dark with thick clouds and drops of rain pelted the windshield. A dreary day to match her mood.

By the time she got done walking Epic and taking her turn in the restroom to change and get ready for the day, the chill and humidity was seeping into her bones. She decided to splurge and go to the little coffee shop she'd seen a few stores down from the diner. Something hot to drink was exactly what she needed to get this day going.

Anna did her best to dry Epic's feet before letting him in the van. There were still dog prints on the floor and blankets. She cringed. There was nothing she could do about it now. Once he was set up, Anna half jogged to the coffee shop and stepped inside.

The intense smells of coffee and pastries filled the air. She inhaled deeply, allowing the fragrance to warm her from the inside out. She wasn't a fan of coffee, but she absolutely loved the smell of it.

She surveyed the small dining area and did a double take. There, sitting at a table near the back, was Joel. Her heart did a cartwheel while her mind insisted she turn around and leave.

Anna considered trying to get hot chocolate to go and ducking back out before he saw her but his head lifted. The instant his eyes locked on hers, there was no going back. She moved in his direction. "Good morning."

"Good morning yourself."

They stared at each other until Anna cleared her throat. "The weather's terrible. It seemed like a good morning for something hot to drink."

"They serve amazing coffee. Their food's pretty good, too." He motioned to the chair opposite him. "You're welcome to join me."

She hesitated and he must have picked up on it.

"I thought we'd agreed on a truce last night." He raised an eyebrow. Then he smiled. It wasn't fair how disarming that mouth of his was. Despite wishing she could've snuck out without him seeing her, Anna began to relax.

"I wouldn't even be in here except Epic insisted I give him some space this morning."

Joel appeared relieved at the change in topic. "He did, huh?"

"Yeah. Between you and me, I think he wanted to commandeer the comforters." She shivered.

Joel laughed then. "It is cold out there."

She sensed he wanted to say something else and was holding back. She appreciated it. "Yeah, it is. I warmed the van up for him. He'll be fine until the sun heats up the air a little. And he does have all the blankets now." She shrugged. "I'll be right back."

Anna headed for the counter and returned a few minutes later, her hands cupping the mug for warmth as she sat down again. "Is this where you got our drinks the other day?" He nodded. "They make a great hot chocolate here." She took another tentative sip.

"Not a coffee drinker?"

"Not usually."

Joel took a sip of his dark brew. "You want any breakfast?"

Anna shook her head. "No, thank you. I had cereal." Which was true, though she'd consider giving her left pinkie for one of those blueberry muffins she'd seen in the display. But she was trying to spend as little as possible to save for a different place to live. The hot chocolate was splurge enough. Before Joel pressed the matter, she asked, "How long have you owned the diner?"

"Almost five years now." He set his mug back down on the table. "Brooke and Chess had their doubts about it, but I was determined. Proved them wrong." He winked.

"That's neat. Good for you. Did you always want to own a diner?"

"Truthfully? No. I woke up one morning and decided I didn't want to work for someone else anymore. I wanted to be my own boss. And everything grew from there. It's one of the best decisions I've ever made." He took another sip of his coffee. "Brooke worries that I work too much. But the diner saved my sanity."

"Oh? How's that?"

Joel ran his fingers through his short hair. She liked the way the front slipped down over his forehead and stopped right above his eyebrows. Anna fought the urge to reach over and brush it back. He seemed to be weighing how much he wanted to tell her. It was the first time she'd seen him hesitate like this. "You don't have to tell me. I shouldn't have asked."

"No, it's not that." He ran a finger down the

handle of his mug. "Life was unpredictable growing up. Money was — scarce. I was always worried about saving money, having a job. This diner has removed most of those concerns."

He'd been staring at the table or through the window right behind Anna while he spoke. Now his gaze sought hers.

The silence grew. The funny thing? It wasn't uncomfortable. Not like it would have been yesterday. Instead, they sipped their drinks and watched as patrons came in and out of the shop.

Joel cleared his throat. "There's a particular question that's been begging for an answer."

Anna's eyebrows drew together. *Uh oh, here it comes.* She knew she shouldn't have started asking personal questions. Now he had one for her. "What's that?"

"Where on earth did you find Epic?"

She laughed, relieved it was a question she could answer. "I'd gone to an office supply store to buy a bunch of stuff, including several boxes of paper. I had the driver's side door open partway while I was loading the boxes into the trunk." She chuckled again at the memory. "I pushed the cart into the corral, turned, and found him sitting behind the wheel in all of his furry glory."

Joel's jaw dropped. "What did you do?"

"You've seen Epic. I was pretty sure he was going to eat me. But he only sat there, his tongue hanging out like he was laughing at me. I tried to get him out of the car and he wouldn't budge. I finally told him, 'If you're not getting out then you need to move over because I'm driving.' And that's exactly what he did. Moved right over to the passenger seat." She gathered some of her hair in one hand. "I put up signs in that parking lot, put an ad in the paper. No one ever contacted me. And by that time, I'd gotten attached to the giant rug."

Joel laughed. Anna had to admit she loved that sound. It was deep and flowed around her like a hug. Without warning, she wondered what it would be like to receive a hug from him.

Surely no one would blame her for the thought. After all, he was incredibly handsome with those dark eyes and strong jaw. She'd found his height to be intimidating when she first met him. But now... Now it was comforting. Combine that with his kindness, and she was drawn to him.

It didn't mean her traitorous heart had to run like a horse galloping across the racetrack, though. She tried to rein in her thoughts to a much safer topic. Something that didn't involve how good-looking her boss was.

Joel glanced at the clock on the wall above the counter of the coffee shop. He was supposed to meet Brooke in about ten minutes so he could help her with some errands. Disappointment about his time here ending was strong.

Anastasia's soft voice brought his attention back to her pretty eyes. "Epic seems to like you. Do you guys have pets? I didn't see any at the cookout yesterday."

"Brooke had rats at one point. Does that count?" Anastasia wrinkled her nose and he laughed loudly. He doubted she had a clue how adorable she was.

"Not a fan of rats?"

"No. Just no."

"Me, either. I felt bad for Brooke when the last one bit the dust. But we voted two to one that she not bring any more into the house."

Anastasia's gaze remained fixed on the wall next to them. "I never had pets growing up. I'm rather enjoying it. Even if Epic is a royal pain sometimes."

"He's a good dog." Joel certainly felt better about knowing she was sleeping in the parking lot with the dog there to protect her. Although Epic had been nothing but friendly to him. He hoped that, if there was a real threat, Epic wouldn't hesitate to take care of the situation.

For the hundredth time, he wanted to know more about her. Where had she moved from? What happened to her? Why doesn't she like to talk about it?

"Anastasia? What are you running from?"

She froze. "Joel, I..."

"Never mind. You don't have to tell me — I shouldn't pry." Joel hoped she would answer. Instead, she twirled a section of hair around her finger, her gaze unfocused.

Awkward silence filled the air until he couldn't take it anymore. He put a hand on her shoulder. "Are you okay?"

She offered him a small smile. "Did you ever go see that other location for your second diner?"

Joel welcomed the change in subject. "Yes, I saw the property Saturday night. It's a great spot, I can't complain about that." He'd talked to everyone at the house about it and none of them would offer their opinions.

"But you're still not sure what to do."

He shook his head.

Anastasia took a drink of her hot chocolate. "Let me ask you this. What about opening another diner is appealing?"

Joel thought about that for a moment. "I guess knowing that I'm doing something to expand. That I'm not standing still. To push myself a little."

"Okay. And the cons?"

"The distance from here to there. Splitting my attention between diners. The cost up front to build it in the first place." Yeah, the cons were definitely outweighing the pros.

"Your diner is obviously popular. You have a loyal customer base. Have you ever considered opening for breakfast?"

Joel thought about that. "I'd entertained the possibility in the beginning, but I chose not to go that route because I didn't know how the diner was going to do."

He focused on Anastasia and caught her grinning. Her dimples winked at him. Goodness, she was beautiful. "What?" He found himself smiling in return.

"It's obviously doing well, maybe the time's right now?"

"Maybe so. It's not a bad idea." He'd have to hire more people, but that wasn't necessarily a bad thing. The hardest adjustment would be not spending the whole day at the diner. Which, according to Chess and Brooke especially, would be good for him.

"Good. I'll expect to see my consulting fee added to my paycheck." Her eyes sparkled.

"How about I buy you breakfast the next time we

bump into each other here? You know, I come by at eight most mornings before work." Joel watched her carefully, half expecting her to object.

Instead, she gave him a shy smile. "I'll keep that in mind. You know, for this being my second day off work, I'm sure seeing my boss a lot."

Joel chuckled. He had no objections.

Chapter Eleven

Liam missed his exit and cursed at the car to his right. He hadn't been able to switch lanes in time. This mess of highways and overpasses in the Dallas/Fort Worth area was a nightmare.

He originally thought he'd get into town and see if he could find any tips on where Anna might have gone next.

He realized now that wasn't going to be possible.

Which meant Rick had better come through with another lead and soon.

Some idiot driver cut him off and he was stuck exiting into downtown Dallas. Liam slammed his palm against the steering wheel. He'd make Anna pay for this crazy search and for taking his thumb drive.

He was going to find her. The longer it took, the less he cared about convincing her to come back to Utah with him. Anna was more trouble than she was worth. He wanted that drive and he'd get it, even if he had to pry it out of her cold, dead fingers.

༚ ♥ ༚

Joel's heart rate jumped when Anastasia breezed into the diner on Tuesday morning. Her hair was loose, flowing like a waterfall down her back. Her dimples appeared when he greeted her.

"Sorry, I'm running a few minutes behind." She gathered her hair and used her fingers to smooth and lift it into a ponytail. "I'm ready for the ground to dry out after the rain yesterday. Epic got into mud this morning. I had to clean him up before I let him into the van. It was a mess." She frowned as she secured the ponytail with a black band.

Watching her fix her hair had him wanting to reach out and run his own fingers through it. He buried his hands in his pockets. He rubbed his thumb over the wooden handle of his knife, each groove familiar to him.

He thought about what she said and tried not to laugh at the picture of Anastasia wrestling with the giant dog over muddy paws. "Did you get him to the groomer?"

"Oh! Yes, and that helped. I can't imagine trying to get all that mud off him if he'd had the longer hair. You won't recognize him next time you see him. I think he lost five pounds." She smiled again. "I guess I'd better get back there and work on the prep."

Joel watched as she disappeared. It was surprising that Courtney wasn't here yet. Five minutes later, his phone rang. When Courtney's voice came over the line, she sounded horrible.

She'd just gotten out of the doctor's office and was told she had strep throat and a sinus infection.

Joel insisted she get some rest and not worry about work. That they had it covered and would hopefully see her in a few days. He couldn't recall the girl calling in sick before. He said a silent prayer that she'd recover quickly.

Courtney's absence meant Anastasia was going to need help to get everything ready for the day.

He heard her working in the back and headed that way. When he rounded the corner, he recognized her at one of the counters, her back to him. "Courtney called..."

Before he got another word out, Anastasia whirled, her hand grasping the handle of a knife. Her eyes widened when she saw it was him.

Joel held up his hands and took a step back. "Whoa. It's only me. I was going to say that Courtney's sick and I'll come back and help you get things ready."

Anastasia's shoulders dropped and she put the knife down with a clatter. "I'm SO sorry."

She turned around again, gripping the edge of the counter with enough force to turn her knuckles white.

What on earth was going on?

Joel approached her carefully until he was by her side. "Are you okay?"

She took in a ragged breath but said nothing.

"Anastasia?"

She folded her arms across her chest, turned, and leaned against the counter. "I didn't hear you come in. You startled me, that's all." She shrugged, as if it hadn't been a big deal.

But Joel could tell by the guarded expression on her face that it was. "Who hurt you?" Because whoever it was had better not show his face around here.

"I'm overreacting." Her hands shook and she was still far paler than normal.

She might be unwilling to share her past, but Joel couldn't take the distress on her face any longer. He turned towards Anastasia and gently pulled her into his arms. He thought she was going to protest and back away. But a heartbeat later, she was leaning against his chest. Joel wrapped his arms around her and rested his cheek against her hair.

It surprised him how right this felt. As if she were made for his arms. His heart pounded hard enough, surely she must hear it.

She slipped her own arms around his waist and sniffed.

More than ever, he wished he knew what had happened to her in the past. He wanted to know what to do to help her feel secure again.

She stepped back and wiped the moisture from her face. "Thanks." Anastasia's eyes focused on everything but him.

Joel cupped her chin and lifted it until she looked at him. "If you ever need someone to talk to, I'm here. I won't say a word to anyone else. That's a promise."

He knew there was a lot she wasn't saying. He'd thought that since the first time he met her. What was she running away from?

He let his arms fall to his side.

"I appreciate that." She moved to the sink and washed her hands. "These tomatoes aren't going to cut themselves." She laughed weakly.

Joel took his cue from her. She was right and the rest of the crew was going to arrive in the next thirty minutes. If it made her feel better to focus on the prep, then that's what they would do.

Anna frowned. How could she let herself fall apart like that? What happened to being strong and not needing another guy again after what Liam did?

Even as she mentally scolded herself, she couldn't deny that she'd felt safer those moments in Joel's arms than she had in a long, long time.

Which was a little scary in and of itself.

Help me to keep my head on straight, God. I don't want to make another mistake.

They worked together to get all the burger fixings prepared. She was hyper aware of his presence, especially when their arms nearly brushed against each other. The mix of pine and spice that was uniquely Joel competed with the smell of the onions he was slicing.

But the silence… it was becoming too much. She cleared her throat. "Sorry for falling apart on you back there."

"You have nothing to apologize for." He turned his head to catch a glimpse of her before going back to slicing onion. "Now I, on the other hand …"

He motioned to the stack of onions, the smell surrounding both of them and finally drowning out the last hint of his cologne. Tears came to their eyes.

Anna chuckled for the first time since everything had happened the day before. "They are incredibly strong today, aren't they? Better you cutting them than me, though I'm not sure it makes a difference if I'm here in the same room."

"I'm not sure, either." He scraped the onion into a food bin and covered them with plastic wrap. Then he deposited the scraps in the trash and washed his hands thoroughly. As soon as that was done, he opened the back door, moving it back and forth in an attempt to get some of the smell out.

Anna was laughing hard now. "As soon as we take that plastic wrap off, we'll be right back to where we started."

"Maybe so. But you do what you can." He winked and she shook her head. "You've got a pretty laugh, Anastasia."

She liked the way her name sounded on his lips. It caused her heart to race. Her cheeks warmed and she whirled to finish the last of the lettuce. The others would be there any minute now.

Joel finally closed the back door again. On his way by to the front of the diner, he lightly placed a hand on her shoulder and gave a gentle squeeze.

The busyness of the day made no difference. All she thought about was the peace she'd experienced while being held in Joel's arms earlier.

కఁ 💜 ఁఖ

Joel tried to be discreet when he drove by Anastasia's van after work. He saw her reading and since he wasn't able to spot Epic, he assumed the dog was lying down. He drove away but stopped the car before leaving the large parking lot. When Anastasia moved her van from the park to the area right next to the diner, Joel felt better. He still hated leaving her there. He'd been working on alternatives the past few days and he had an idea.

He needed to run it past Brooke first.

When he got home, Joel found her in her room.

She motioned him inside as soon as he approached. "What's up, Joel?"

"Do you have a minute?"

"Sure. Should I be worried?"

"No. But I was wondering if you'd made a decision about whether you were going to move out."

"I'd like to. But I don't want to go to an apartment. Not after living someplace roomy like this. I've been searching and I can't quite afford a rental house, either." She released a sigh of frustration as she sank onto her bed. "No, I haven't figured out what I'm going to do yet."

"Well, I may have an idea that might benefit two people at one time."

Brooke's eyes brightened with interest. "Go on."

Joel put an elbow on her dresser. "Do you remember Anna? She came to the cookout."

"Yes, I remember her. I got to talk to her some. She seemed nice. Quiet."

"That's her. She needs to find a place to rent as well and was hoping to find something next month. However, her situation has changed and she needs to get into someplace as soon as possible." He paused. "If the two of you rented a two-bedroom house, you'd avoid the apartment thing and you'd both be able to afford it."

He could tell by Brooke's face that she liked the idea.

"Have you mentioned this to Anna yet?"

"No. I wanted to talk to you, first." He'd been praying that, if this was the answer to both of their problems, that things would come together smoothly. "And you ladies would have a built-in security system with her dog."

"Oh! That's right. Boy, he's huge. And I'll bet he's hairy." Brooke fidgeted with the hem of her quilt.

"Yeah, he is. But Anastasia had the dog's hair cut short yesterday. It's totally up to you, though. I don't want you in any situation you're uncomfortable with. She works hard and she's reliable. That says a lot about her."

Brooke stared at the wall thoughtfully. "Would you bring it up to her? See how she reacts? This might be a good solution for both of us."

"If you're sure, I'll talk to her tomorrow."

"Thanks, Joel." She stood and gave him a hug.

"You're welcome. Hang in there, huh?"

She took a step back and smiled. "Will do."

❧ 🖤 ❧

By the next morning, Joel had gone over a dozen different ways to bring the idea up with Anastasia. She seemed reluctant to let anyone help her and he didn't want her to think this was some kind of charity.

He headed to the coffee shop like he always did, surprised and pleased to find Anastasia already at the table they'd shared last week. "Hey, you! Good morning."

"Hey." She was holding a mug of hot chocolate in her slender hands.

"I'm going to grab me some coffee. Muffins: Chocolate chip or blueberry?"

"Oh, you don't need to get anything for me."

He hiked up an eyebrow and pinned her with mock-seriousness. "Chocolate chip or blueberry?"

"Blueberry, please."

"Coming right up."

When he got back to their table, he slid the plate holding her muffin over to her.

"Thank you." Her cheeks flushed and she immediately pulled the paper away from the base of the muffin. "I have to admit that dry cereal is getting a bit old."

Joel laughed. "I imagine so. And you're welcome." He smiled at her before taking a large bite of his own chocolate chip muffin.

His phone rang and he answered it. When the conversation was over, he hung up. "Courtney's still sick. She sounded terrible. I told her to take as long as she needed."

Anastasia grimaced. "I sympathize. With classes, too, I'm sure she's stressed."

"I'm hoping she'll be back to her old self again soon."

"Me, too."

Joel thought this was as good a time as any to bring up the rental house idea. He said a prayer for the right words and that, if it was something God wanted to happen, that he would soften Anastasia's heart to the idea. It was hard enough when she got upset last time, he didn't want to repeat the experience.

"I wanted to run something by you."

That had her immediate attention. She focused

her green eyes on his face. "What's up?"

"Brooke is considering moving out. I think that sometimes being the only female in the house gets a bit much. She doesn't want to get an apartment, but houses are over her price limit. She's thinking of finding a roommate." He paused, trying to gauge her reaction thus far and wasn't having much luck. "I thought about you. The two of you could rent a two-bedroom house, split the cost. If you find something with a yard, you'd have a great place for Epic, too."

Anastasia put down her muffin, leaned back in her chair, and gave him a pointed stare. "I told you, I don't need or want charity. I'm doing fine. I thought we'd gotten past this."

The hurt in her eyes pained Joel, but he wasn't going to let this go. She needed to get out of that van and somewhere safer. The days would get warmer soon as spring approached. She couldn't leave Epic in the van for long once they did.

"Now, hold on. This is different. You said you were going to be searching for an apartment or a place to rent when you had the money." She didn't look at all convinced but at least she hadn't stood to leave yet. "This is no different. I'm informing you of a possible opportunity to do exactly that — and earlier than you'd hoped for." Joel watched her, dared her to contradict the truth of his words.

What if she got angry and walked out? Parked her van in a different location? What if she quit her job? Panic filled him as the thoughts pummeled his mind from every direction. He'd known her a week and already he couldn't picture his life without her in it.

The realization startled him.

Joel didn't want to lose her. But he also needed to fix her situation. It was worth the risk of making her angry if it meant she was somewhere safe and warm.

He watched as emotions paraded across her face and prayed she'd give the idea some thought before making a decision.

Chapter Twelve

Anna narrowed her gaze, but Joel kept his eyes on her without flinching. She mulled over his words. He was right. While she would like to rent something without a roommate, it was going to be awhile before she could afford it.

But if she went into renting a house with Brooke, there was a possibility she'd be out of the van in a week or so.

The idea was more than appealing.

"I'm sorry for the knee-jerk reaction. I've been in a position before where someone helped me and then insisted I was indebted." She stopped there, not wanting to give anything else away and hoping she hadn't done so already. "I don't want to do that again." She chewed on her bottom lip. "I doubt Brooke would want to put up with Epic."

"I told her you cut his hair shorter to keep the shedding down. She likes animals a lot. She wouldn't mind. And he's a built-in security system.

You can't go wrong there."

"True." She put a finger on her chin. "It would depend on the rent. But a house would be much better than an apartment." She shrugged. "I'd like to talk to Brooke myself and make sure she's okay with Epic. But it's definitely something I'm interested in."

A grin spread across Joel's face. "Great! Do you want to come over for dinner tonight so you two can talk about it?"

"Sure. That would be fine."

"Okay, I'll let Brooke know. I'm not sure what we'll eat, but it won't be hamburgers."

Anna half expected Joel to gloat over the fact that she'd expressed interest in the idea. But he gave her a genuine smile and seemed pleased that she'd agreed to speak to Brooke.

Anna finished the last bite of her muffin and wadded up her napkin. She'd barely put it on the plate when Joel took it to the counter for her.

She watched him as he worked. The man was thoughtful. A gentleman. She suppressed a smile thinking about how he'd insisted on buying the muffin. She was glad he had. When she got into a rental, she'd find a recipe and make a bunch of those herself.

Was it possible that he was simply interested in being her friend? That he didn't have some kind of agenda?

"It's almost nine. We'd better get to the diner." Joel held her chair out while she stood. "There are people in this town counting the minutes until they come in for lunch." He winked.

"You bet. Let's go save the world, one cheeseburger at a time." Anna gave him a small smile and followed him through the coffee shop. He opened the door for her and she stepped out into the cool air.

They continued silently to the diner and then inside. Joel turned the lights on while Anna headed to the back to begin prepping for the day.

Twenty minutes later, Joel joined her. "I called Brooke and she's thrilled you're coming over tonight. She said she's already found several houses that might work. I think she considered calling the realtor and seeing if you guys could tour them tomorrow, but was afraid she was jumping the gun a little." He chuckled.

Anna definitely wanted to talk to Brooke first. But the more she thought about the possible situation, the better she felt about it. In fact, it was the first time in a long while that she felt completely at peace with the direction things were going. "Can you text her and tell her that's a great idea?" She shot Joel a look from the corner of her eye. "The sooner I get out of the van the better. I'm going to be finding mud in everything for a while."

"I sure can." He seemed pleased as he typed a message to Brooke. When he was finished, his expression became serious. "I want to make it perfectly clear that you are never indebted to me. For any reason."

His words touched Anna's heart. "I appreciate that. Thank you."

"You are an amazing employee. For that alone, I owe you."

She felt a pang of disappointment. He was only referring to their working relationship. That's all there was anyway, right? If that was true, why did it bother her? She shook her head, trying to dismiss the flood of confusing emotions. "You pay me a good wage. You owe me nothing. Other than my paychecks." She did her best to keep the conversation light.

Joel laughed. "It's not just that. I..." He paused, the tips of his ears turning red. She thought he was going to change his mind and not speak but he finally turned to face her directly. "Anastasia, I enjoy spending time with you. A lot. It's quickly become the best part of my day."

Anna's eyes widened. Her blood raced, pulsing loud enough that she heard the rush in her ears. She realized suddenly that seeing him had become one of hers as well. Without thought, her feet moved and took her a step closer to him. What was she doing? She needed to get back to prep. Or excuse herself. Something!

Joel extended a finger and swept some of her hair away from her face, depositing it behind her ear. "It's even softer than I thought it'd be," he murmured. When she didn't move, Joel brushed her cheek with the back of his fingers. His gaze shifted from her eyes to her lips.

They heard the front door swing open. Anna and Joel stepped apart simultaneously and she turned back towards the counter as Adam entered. He greeted them both and then he and Joel went up to the front.

Anna released a shaky breath. With her hands braced against the counter, she tried to calm her racing heart. Call her crazy, but if Adam hadn't come in then, she thought Joel might have kissed her.

Somehow, she was both disappointed and relieved that he didn't. What did that say about her?

❧ ♥ ❧

Anastasia remained on Joel's mind for the rest of the day. If it hadn't been for Adam's untimely arrival, Joel had no doubt he'd have been kissing her. He regretted that he hadn't had the chance.

Since then, it seemed like everything conspired against him having a real opportunity to talk to her. Was she okay? Or had he spooked her? But all he could do was anticipate seeing her at dinner tonight.

Brooke had texted him to say she'd contacted the realtor and already had an appointment to view several properties tomorrow evening.

After Anastasia's shift was over, she promised to meet him at the house in a half hour. Joel raced home to give himself time to change clothes and make sure the backyard was set up for Epic. He'd barely accomplished all that when her green van pulled up in front of the house.

He watched as she stepped down, closely followed by her giant dog. She saw him and gave him a little wave.

Joel smiled and held the gate open for them. Epic acted like he owned the place and trotted right into the backyard.

Anastasia shook her head good-naturedly. "He likes it here."

She passed him on the way through the gate and he caught a whiff of citrus. He liked the way she smelled. He could still feel the way her hair had glided across his finger.

He secured the gate and led her around to the back door. "Brooke can't wait to talk to you about the houses she's seen online. I've been hearing all about it every time Chess is out of earshot."

"Why doesn't she want to talk about it when he's there?"

"He's not real happy about her moving out. He'd rather we all stayed together. I'm not even sure what all's going on in his head right now." He paused. "I'm glad you're here, Anastasia." The others were waiting just inside, otherwise he might have stayed outside to talk to her for a few minutes.

"Me, too."

Epic seemed content and they went inside.

"Hello, Anna." Chess greeted her from the living room. "It's nice to see you again."

"You, too." Anastasia nodded to him. "I hope your week was a good one."

Chess smiled. "It's been long already. I go to Dallas Monday and Tuesday and this week we had a lot of bugs to work out. I'm glad I could work from home today. The rest of the week should be better."

Brooke peeked around the corner and waved to them over the bar. "Come on in and make yourself at home, Anna."

"Thanks! Do you need any help in there?"

"Nah, I've got it covered. I'll be out in a second."

Everyone in the living room found a spot to sit. Anna ended up next to Joel on the couch. That her pulse quickened was not lost on her. There was a sound at the sliding glass door and Chess chuckled when they spotted Epic watching them.

"I think he'd like to be inside," he commented.

"Epic would like to be a lap dog," Anna muttered. "He's spoiled." She almost commented on him sleeping with her every night but she didn't know if Joel had told the rest of the family she was sleeping in her van. If he hadn't, she'd rather not volunteer the information.

Brooke made good on her promise and joined them, sitting on the couch on the other side of Joel. "I'm glad you could come. I hope you like chicken Alfredo and breadsticks."

"Are you kidding? It smells amazing." Anna's stomach let out a long growl. "As I was saying."

The room erupted in laughter.

Chess smiled at Brooke. "Don't worry, my stomach has the same reaction to Brooke's cooking."

Brooke seemed embarrassed by the wink or the comment, Anna wasn't sure which. But Brooke's mouth widened with a grin at the same time.

Anna waved towards the kitchen. "Well, I can't wait. And seriously, if there's anything I can do to help, let me know."

"You spent the day cooking and serving food for this slave driver." Brooke elbowed Joel. "I wouldn't dream of putting you to work here. Relax and take the night off."

Anna had to admit that sounded nice.

They all chatted for a while before Brooke disappeared into the kitchen again. Her voice occasionally floated over the bar when she had a comment to make.

Anna had decided that everyone in the household seemed great when she came for the cookout. But now that she had another chance to chat with them, she liked them even more. Chess and Joel were very much opposites. Where Chess was quiet, Joel was outgoing.

Chess didn't speak much, but he seemed kind. And immensely more serious than the other two put together.

And Joel? Well, he was being a gentleman. He made sure she had something to drink and that she was included in the conversation. He even went outside to check on Epic once and get the dog water.

It wasn't long before Brooke told them it was time to eat. She had everything out on the table.

The Alfredo was perfect, complete with tender chicken, small pieces of tomato, and creamy sauce. Even the breadsticks were sprinkled liberally with garlic and Parmesan cheese. The whole meal was mouth-watering.

If things worked out and she and Brooke did end up roommates, she might have to get Brooke to share some of her recipes. Anna could cook, but preferred to bake. Between the two of them, they should have no problem staying fed.

Conversation flowed through dinner. When they were done eating, Brooke stood. "Why don't you guys go play a video game or something? Anna and I are going to take care of these dishes and talk shop a bit."

Anna didn't miss how Chess frowned and disappeared from the room before anyone else had gotten up from their chairs. She hoped he didn't disagree with her and Brooke being roommates.

Joel must have noticed the uncertainty on her face. He leaned close and spoke low near her ear.

"It's complicated and has nothing to do with you."

Shivers traveled down her spine at the sensation of his breath gliding across her cheek. She moved away quickly, hoping he didn't notice her reaction.

Seriously, ever since what she thought was a near kiss this morning, it was like her body was attuned to everything he was doing.

He moved away from her and into the living room. Anna helped Brooke collect the dishes from the table and carry them into the kitchen.

It wasn't until they were busy washing them that the subject of a rental house came up. They spoke at length, comparing everything from how clean they preferred their living spaces to be to how they'd split electricity and water.

Anna heard Epic bark from the backyard. "I don't mind leaving him outside during the day when I'm gone. But I'd prefer he be indoors otherwise. I realize he's a large dog. Will that be a problem at all?"

Brooke looked thoughtful. "He seems like a sweetie. I don't mind as long as we keep up with the vacuuming and you take care of the pet deposit."

"Of course." Anna wouldn't have dreamed of letting Brooke chip in on the deposit. And at her previous apartment, she vacuumed several times a week to keep the dog hair at a minimum. "Does that mean we're going to do this?"

The corners of Brooke's mouth curled up. "I'm comfortable with the idea. You?" Anna nodded and Brooke motioned for her to follow. "I took the liberty of searching for houses that are available not far from here. I figured it would be better for you to stay close to the diner. And I don't want to be far from the guys or the salon where I work. Don't tell Chess I said that. He'll assume it's all because of him."

Anna made a motion of zipping her lips shut and tossing the invisible key over her shoulder. "Did you find anything?" She followed Brooke upstairs to her bedroom.

Brooke opened her laptop and clicked on the web browser. "I did! There are a couple of two-bedroom houses and the rent is reasonable. If we split it, we shouldn't have any problem. I called and they will let you have Epic. I've got an appointment set up with a realtor tomorrow at six-thirty. She'll show us around and if we like a house, we'll be able to sign the application papers on the spot." Brooke's voice rose with excitement.

Her enthusiasm was catching. They browsed through pictures of the rental homes Brooke found.

One in particular had a six-foot wooden fence surrounding the backyard. That was the one Anna hoped they'd like because it would be perfect for Epic.

Anna stifled a yawn and checked her watch. "Wow, it's getting late. I'd better get going. Brooke, thank you for a great dinner. I'm excited about the houses tomorrow."

"You're welcome and I am, too!"

They walked back downstairs where Anna wrote her phone number down for Brooke in case plans changed. She was supposed to meet Brooke at their house and they'd ride over together. Anna was assured that Epic could remain in the backyard while they were gone.

Anna liked Brooke. She had a feeling their personalities would mesh well. Maybe they could even be friends. Gee, what a novel idea.

Joel stood when they entered the living room. There was still no sign of Chess.

Joel motioned to the back door. "I'll walk you out."

She said her goodbyes and then stepped through the door Joel held open and into the waiting tongue of Epic. Her dog acted as though he hadn't seen her in a week, running around her and bathing her arms. "Yes, I missed you, too. Come on, big guy. Let's go home."

Home. She might have a real one soon. The thought elicited a smile.

"What are you so happy about?" Joel's deep voice rumbled at her side.

"I think things are going to work out. I'm looking forward to actually having a home to go to."

He nudged her gently with his elbow. "I'll sleep better at night knowing you're not in your van, too."

Anna tilted her head up at him, unsure of what to say to that.

He led the way to the van. Anna let Epic in and then walked around to the driver's door. Joel followed. "I'm glad you and Brooke get along."

Anna smiled at him. "Me, too. Thanks for your part in pulling things together."

"You're welcome." Joel studied her face, his dark eyes a mix of emotions. "Anastasia?"

"Yes?"

"Will you have breakfast with me tomorrow?"

"I'm here late tonight and then I'll see you at work. Aren't you worried you'll get tired of me?"

"Not even remotely."

His response sent another string of shivers up

and down her spine. That in combination with the way he was watching her — as if he didn't want her to drive away — made it impossible to refuse.

"I'll be at the coffee shop at eight."

"Good." Joel opened the door for her. "Stay safe."

"I will." She had to pass close enough to him getting into the van that her shoulder brushed against his chest. She got settled in her chair. "Good night."

"Good night." Joel closed the door for her and took several steps back.

When she checked the rear-view mirror, she saw that he remained there until she'd driven out of sight.

She blew out a lungful of air, the windshield fogging over. She turned the heater on full blast to clear it.

She'd basically agreed to a breakfast date.

The realization resulted in a war between nerves, anticipation, and confusion.

The interest definitely went both ways. But it was complicated. He was her boss. She was going to be roommates with his sort-of sister.

And there was Liam. Joel still knew nothing about her ex-boss and ex-boyfriend. What would he think if he did?

Chapter Thirteen

Joel got to the coffee shop fifteen minutes early and claimed a table close to the window where he could watch for Anastasia. The moment he saw her, his heart raced like a freight train. He stood when she approached the table. "Good morning."

"Good morning." She flashed a bright smile at him and slid into her seat.

Those dimples. He never grew tired of seeing them. "We enjoyed having you over for dinner last night."

"I think it wore Epic out. He was snoring when I left."

Joel pictured the dog lying on his back in the van, tongue lolling to one side, snores filling the space. It brought out a bark of laughter. "Did you get any rest?"

"Not as much as I do most nights."

Yeah, he hadn't slept well, either. His mind kept going through the reasons why he continuously felt himself drawn to the beautiful woman sitting across from him. The sun filtered through the window and brought out the highlights in her hair. She wore a green shirt that seemed to take her eyes and brighten them up even more.

She was drop-dead gorgeous. But it wasn't only that. The way she approached the challenges in her life impressed him. Most people he knew would be complaining up one side and down the other if they had to sleep in a van for even one night. Much less for over a week. He admired her.

And he was glad that she'd hopefully be in a rental house with Brooke before long. He hadn't been teasing about sleeping better when she was no longer staying in a parking lot.

"What would you like for breakfast? I'm buying. No arguments."

Anastasia raised an eyebrow, the corners of her mouth lifting slightly. "Hot chocolate. And surprise me with a pastry. Anything will be fine."

"You've got it."

The coffee shop was unusually busy today for some reason. He returned with her drink and set it down in front of her. "Okay, choices are a little different today. I got two things and you pick whichever you want. I'm good with either." He slid the food onto the table. "We've got a peach scone and a wild berry muffin."

"Oooh! Those both sound good."

"In that case." He produced a plastic knife he'd snagged along with napkins. "How about we split them?"

Her face lit up. "That sounds perfect. Thank you."

Joel cut both pastries in half, handed her a napkin, and reclaimed his seat.

Anastasia took a bite of the scone. "Yep, that's amazing." She groaned and took another bite. When she'd swallowed, she spoke again. "I get that Chess would rather Brooke not move out. But I'm guessing there's more to it than that."

"Ah. Yeah, I'm trying to sort out the same thing." He took a sip of coffee and set the mug down. "They both have strong personalities. And when we first all found each other, we kind of settled into our places in the family. Chess was the protector while Brooke was encouraging and nurturing. And I tried to fix everything and make sure we all stayed together."

"Maybe he doesn't feel like he'll be able to protect her if she leaves."

"I'm pretty sure you're right about that. I'm not keen on seeing her leave, either. But I want her to be happy." Joel frowned. "I just hope Chess gets used to the idea. They aren't talking as much as they normally do."

"That's sad." Anastasia seemed thoughtful.

"They've always been good friends. I don't want to see anything get in the way of that." He studied Anastasia across the table. "You don't have any siblings?"

"No. No close family." She hesitated, as if trying to decide how much to tell him. "I have no idea who my father is. My mother was young when she had me and the responsibility was too much. My grandparents took me in and raised me. They passed and I never got to know any of the extended family." There wasn't even a hint of sadness in her eyes, only acceptance for what was. "You're lucky to have Chess and Brooke."

"Yeah, I am." Joel swallowed hard and reached over to cover her hand with his. "Because of them, I'm not alone now. I'm sorry you've spent some of your life that way." He wanted to tell her that she had him. That she wasn't alone anymore.

Anastasia shrugged. "It is what it is." She turned her head towards the window.

She sounded nonchalant but Joel didn't buy it. In general, people were social beings and not meant to be on their own. No matter the circumstances that led them here, he was grateful that God had brought Chess and Brooke into his life. And now Anastasia. He lightly ran his thumb over the backs of her fingers, the soft skin a little cool to the touch.

She swung her gaze from the window to where their hands touched. Then, slowly, up to his face. He gave her a smile and her hand a gentle squeeze before going back to his breakfast.

When her cheeks took on a light pink hue, he was pretty certain she reacted as much to him as he did to her. The whole idea was both exhilarating and scary at the same time.

Joel motioned to her empty plate. "You finished?"

"Yes. Thank you again, it was wonderful."

"You're welcome." He cleared their table. Their hour had evaporated in what seemed like minutes and they needed to get to the diner. He was determined to ask her out on a real date soon — when they both were off work and able to spend an entire afternoon and evening together.

The thought made him smile. Hopefully, when

the time was right, she would agree to the date.

Anna and Joel left the coffee shop together. There was definitely something changing between them. She sensed it every time they spoke, now. She was becoming more relaxed around him, despite every attempt to keep the distance.

Had it truly been just over a week since he first met her? It seemed like a great deal longer. As if she'd escaped from a nightmare and found solace in a bubble that remained impervious to the stresses of the rest of the world.

She rather liked her new life here.

They approached the diner as Courtney came into view with a grin on her face.

Joel waved. "There's the slacker. How're you doing?"

"Other than tiring easy, I'm back to normal. That was a rough one."

They moved as a group towards the back door of the diner.

Joel put a hand out to stop them.

"What's wro…" Anna's eyes followed his gaze. Gouges marred the surface of the door along the edge near the handle. Someone had tried to get into the diner.

Had Liam found her? Surely, if he had, he wouldn't have wasted his time trying to break into the place she worked. He'd go after her while she was alone somewhere.

She jogged away from the store far enough to see her van. It seemed to be okay, though she couldn't see Epic from there.

When Anna returned to the others, Joel was reaching out to pull the handle down.

"It's still locked. Whoever tried to get inside wasn't successful." He pulled his phone out. "I'm still going to report it in case someone tries this again." Joel focused on Anna, his eyes holding questions he didn't voice.

She had an idea what he was asking and shook her head. She'd heard nothing at all last night and she'd been parked near the diner.

Courtney crossed her arms and leaned against the brick wall of the building.

Anna only half listened to the conversation Joel was having with the police station. The hair on the back of her neck stood on end and she found herself glancing around, as if the person who did this might be there watching them.

Panic welled up in her chest. She tried to swallow it down. This wasn't like the advertising agency. This had nothing at all to do with her.

A hand cupped her elbow and she jumped.

Joel's concerned face came into focus. "Anastasia? Are you okay?"

She bobbed her head, quite certain she wasn't the least bit convincing. When did he get off the phone?

"They said it's okay to go inside if we're certain no one broke into the place. They're going to come down and take pictures of the damage for the record in case something like this happens again. I can file with the insurance company for a repair if needed." He looked thoughtful. "From now on, why don't you two come to the front door? I'll open it for you. It's much more visible. I'd be more comfortable with that at this point."

Courtney and Anna agreed simultaneously.

Once they entered, Joel went through the diner to make sure everything was in its place. He gave Anna and Courtney the go ahead to get started with the preparations, saying he was going to go out and take a few pictures of the damage himself before the police officer arrived.

By the time the police had finished their report, the rest of his crew had arrived. The day was in full swing, but Anna couldn't shake the panic that filled her when she'd first seen the door. *God, please keep us safe from whoever it was that tried to break in.*

Anna arrived at Brooke's house exactly at six-thirty. Once she got the dog settled, she climbed into Brooke's car and they headed to the first house where the realtor said she'd meet them.

Anna couldn't stop the thrum of excitement at the idea of getting out of the van and into a place with more space. "I'm afraid I won't have much in the way of furniture to contribute."

"It'll be fine. I don't have a lot, either. We'll hit up the thrift shops and garage sales." Brooke checked her rear-view mirror and changed lanes. "It'll be an adventure."

Yes, and one Anna looked forward to embarking on. If she had to, she was sure she'd be able to pick up an air mattress or something like that to sleep on. It had to be more comfortable than the van seat.

The rental houses they toured were all within ten minutes of either the diner or the house Brooke shared with the guys. While all three were nice, it was the second one that both of them kept talking about.

The fact that the house was in a decent neighborhood and had the lowest rent solidified the decision for them. After talking alone, they informed the realtor that they'd like to rent the house. Before leaving the third house, they filled out the application the realtor gave them and said they should hear back sometime tomorrow. The house was empty and the owner was in a hurry for it to be occupied again.

Back at Brooke's house, all four of them sat in the living room while the women told the guys about the rental they'd chosen.

Brooke showed pictures from her smart phone. The phone had been passed around the room more times than Anna could count.

"It's a good neighborhood," Chess said. They were the first words he'd spoken since they started telling the guys about the house. "If you two get the house, I'll come by and make sure a motion light is installed by the front door."

"Thanks, Chess. That would be great." Brooke looked pleased.

Anna was fascinated as she watched the family dynamics. The guys suggested different things they should ask about and Brooke added them all to a list on her phone.

At that moment, there was a knock at the door. Epic took the liberty to bark from the backyard and everyone laughed.

"I ordered pizza," Joel said as he stood. "Anastasia, you're welcome to stay and eat with us."

"Are you sure? I don't want to interrupt."

Everyone else assured her it was fine. While Joel went to get the pizza from the delivery man, Brooke turned to Anna. "I think it's sweet he calls you that. It's a pretty name."

"Thank you." Anna had never thought so. Until the first time Joel had used it. He made it sound pretty. She pushed the thought aside before she blushed, something she was doing far too often while around him. A small smile played at her lips while she gathered with the others in the kitchen.

By the time they'd eaten dinner and visited for a while, it was ten in the evening. "I'd better get going," Anna told them. "But I had a lot of fun tonight. Thanks for letting me stay and eat with you all."

"Anytime," Brooke assured her. "I don't know about you, but I can't wait to hear back from the realtor."

"Me, either." Anna grinned. "I'll see you all soon. Have a great rest of your weekend."

Joel joined her. "I'll walk you out." He held up a paper towel containing several pizza crusts. "Besides, it's only fair that Epic gets his share of dinner."

After Epic gulped down the food, Anna opened the van door and let him in. She closed it again and turned to face Joel. "Your family is great. I had a lot of fun."

"I'm glad. I did, too." Joel gestured towards the van. "I promised I wouldn't say anything. But after someone tried to break into the diner... I'd rather you didn't sleep in the parking lot." His eyes pleaded with her. "Please consider staying here. It's only for a couple of days until you and Brooke get into a house. Epic can hang out in the backyard instead of having to stay in the van tomorrow. Plus, tonight's likely the last major cold front. It's supposed to dip down close to freezing."

Anna shook her head and from his expression, he'd expected it. "I'm not comfortable with that, Joel." She wanted to be annoyed at him for even bringing it up, except that she was dreading spending the night there herself. And she could tell by Joel's expression that he was more than worried. He looked desperate.

Joel didn't like talking about what happened to his parents. But right now, he needed to make sure Anastasia was somewhere safe. Between the attempted break-in and the near-freezing temperatures, he had to do something. "Do you mind if we sit down and talk for a minute?"

Anastasia agreed and he took her hand, leading her to the front steps. They sat down side-by-side. Joel didn't want to release her hand — it felt too wonderful in his — but he did and turned to see her face.

"I realize I'm being pushy. Maybe where you stay tonight is none of my business." He dreaded putting a voice to his memories. "I had amazing parents. But we grew up poor. Like, sometimes we lived in our car poor. But no matter what, they made sure I got to school and that I had meals. I know they went without regularly."

He paused, pulling memories together. He

withdrew his pocket knife and ran his thumb over the handle. "One day in the middle of winter, I was at school. It snowed— set all kinds of records with ice and accumulation. I was safe and warm at the school all day. But my parents... They tried to stay warm with the car running, but the snow eventually blocked the exhaust pipe."

He heard Anastasia gasp but he kept his eyes on a moth that kept flying around them. "They both died that day from the fumes. Though someone told me at the time they might have died from exposure if that hadn't gotten them first. I didn't have any extended family willing to take me in. I entered the foster care system then and remained until I aged out at eighteen. The last placement with the Ziegler family — that's where I met Brooke. Then Chess soon after we moved out. God brought us together and if he hadn't... I don't even want to know where we'd all be now."

"Wow." A soft sigh escaped her lips but she said nothing else. Her eyes brimmed with tears and she studied her own hands closely. "Your dad gave you that knife, didn't he?"

Joel nodded and took in a steadying breath. "It reminds me of him. Of the hours I spent watching him carve when I was a kid." He slipped it back into his pocket. "What happened to my parents — that's why knowing you're sleeping out there bothers me so much. Especially on a cold night like tonight. Maybe my fear is irrational, but every fiber in my being objects to it."

"I can't even imagine. I'm sorry for your loss, Joel. I get what you're saying. I do. If it helps, I'm nervous about staying there tonight, too. Not because of the cold, but after someone tried to get into the diner." She absently took a section of hair and twirled it around her finger. "Does your family know I live in a van right now?"

Joel cringed. "Yeah, they know. I didn't tell them directly but they figured it out. Besides, we recognized the situation. Most of us have been in a similar one in the past."

Anastasia closed her eyes, the corners of her mouth dipping low in a frown. Was she praying? Thinking? She finally opened them again and stared at him. "I'm not comfortable staying in your house. Any other suggestions?"

"Park in our driveway. I'll leave the back door unlocked in case you need anything. If you get cold, and you change your mind, you'll have options."

There wasn't anything else to say. It was up to Anastasia. All he could do was pray that she would either accept the offer, or that God give him the peace to get through the night.

He didn't think she was going to answer. Finally, she said, "Okay. For tonight, anyway."

Chapter Fourteen

"You like her, don't you?"

Brooke's voice startled Joel when he re-entered the house. He pressed his hand to his chest and leaned against a wall. "Are you trying to give me a heart attack?" He shot her a look of mild annoyance.

"Sorry." She didn't sound convincing. "And I'm not going to let you change the subject, either."

Joel moved to the kitchen where they were less likely to be overheard. "Yeah, I like her." He ran a hand over his chin. "And I convinced her to park her van here in case it got too cold. It's definitely safer here."

"Good. I'm glad. I can imagine how awkward this whole thing is. I hope we hear from the realtor tomorrow and get into a house soon." Brooke pressed a finger to her temple.

"What's your opinion of her?"

Brooke leaned against the counter. "She's sweet. I think you two are good for each other." She paused.

"But?"

"There's something about her that she's holding back. I have no idea what."

He knew exactly what she meant. Anastasia was reluctant to talk about her past. That she'd opened up as much as she had was a big step.

He realized Brooke was watching him. That's something he had always appreciated about her. She let him process. Oh, she also peppered him with questions later, but she gave him the time he needed to think through things. "Do you have any reservations about having Anastasia for a roommate?"

"None. I have a good feeling about it. This is going to work out well."

"I agree." He paused. "I want to spend time with her. Outside the diner. I thought I'd ask her to go on a picnic once you two get settled."

"You want to take her on a date." Brooke's smile was brilliant and she straightened away from the counter.

"Yeah, I do." He thought about it and chuckled. "This is crazy, isn't it?"

Brooke put an arm around his neck and hugged him for a moment. "She's a lucky girl, Joel. Don't you forget that." She gave him a quick peck on the cheek and left.

Anna did sleep better parked out in front of Joel's house than she would have at the diner. It was a lot quieter, too. But when she woke up, the last thing she intended to do was knock on the door to use their restroom or shower. Afraid that Joel would be worried if he saw the van was gone, she wrote a note thanking them all for their kindness and then said she'd see him at work.

Besides, after sleeping in her clothes, she wasn't real keen on anyone seeing her as a rumpled mess. Joel in particular.

After leaving the note on the front door, she stopped at a park to let Epic out for a bit and then the truck stop for a shower.

She'd hoped to wait until Sunday to do laundry, but the rain the other day made that impossible. She was running out of clothes, so she made a stop at the laundromat.

Since the day was cool, she opted to let Epic stay in the van instead of leaving him in Joel's backyard. It would hopefully be only another day or two.

By the time she entered the diner, Joel was in the front and she heard Courtney singing in the back.

"Hey there, stranger." Joel's eyes lit up. "Are you doing okay this morning?"

"I'm good. Thank you again. I hadn't realized how loud the roads are in this area of town until I wasn't trying to sleep through them." Anna chuckled. "I'd better get back there and help her."

She sensed him watching her until she got into the back.

All morning, Anna checked her phone to make sure she hadn't missed a call from the realtor or Brooke. The call didn't come through until she was out strolling with Epic on her break after lunch.

"Hello?"

"Hey, Anna. It's Brooke. The realtor called. We got the house! Not only that, but we can go by and sign the papers today before six. If we bring the deposits and rent, they'll let us move in tomorrow!"

Wow. She'd hoped for quick, but even this was more than she'd expected. "This is amazing."

"I know! I'll call around and see if it's possible to have the water and power turned on over there today. Will you be able to meet me at the realtor's office at five to make sure we have enough time? I'm sure Joel won't mind."

"I'll double-check with him, but that'll be great."

They talked about money and how much they each needed to bring with them.

By the time Anna got back to the diner, she was practically floating on air. Only one more night in her van.

"What's that grin for?" Joel asked when he saw her, a smile of his own lighting his face.

"Brooke and I got the house and we can move in tomorrow." She forced a neutral expression. "That is, of course, if I convince my boss to let me leave at 4:45 so I can sign those papers at 5:00. He's a real stickler on the hours, you know."

"Oh is he, now?" Humor twinkled in Joel's eyes. He glanced over at the handful of customers eating in the dining area. "I suppose that can be arranged." He flashed a smile her way. "I'm happy for you both. I'll arrange for Saturday off for both of us to help get you ladies moved in."

Anna wanted to object. Mostly because she desperately needed the money. But getting moved in and everything settled would be good. She didn't have much to carry into the house, but she imagined Brooke could use the help. "That'd be great. Thanks, Joel. For everything."

"You're welcome."

His smile warmed her as she got back to work. *Thank you, Father, for leading me here and providing a place for Epic and me to live.*

✥

When Joel arrived at Brooke and Anna's new house, he saw that both gals were already unloading items from their vehicles.

Chess drove up and parked right behind Joel. Both men got out.

"The tree is nice," Chess commented, his mouth turning down at the corners.

Joel agreed. The oak stood tall with branches that stretched over the roof. Once the leaves came in, it would be a fantastic source of shade this summer. He was concerned about Chess and knew getting Brooke moved in was hard for him to do. Joel admired him for stepping up and helping anyway.

Epic's insistent barks floated to him from the backyard. There was scratching at the fence and then the top of the dog's head became visible.

Brooke opened the front door and stepped out. "Hey, you two. Thanks for helping. You guys want the quick tour before bringing things in?" Her eyes lit up as she ushered them inside.

Joel followed her through the large living room, kitchen with small attached dining area, two bedrooms, and the bathroom.

At Anna's bedroom, she waved at them and smiled. "What do you think? A step up from my previous place of residence, right?"

She appeared content. Happy. Joel grinned in response. "I'd definitely say you've upgraded." He gave her a wink. "Do you need any help getting your things inside?"

"No, but thank you. I've got almost everything. It didn't take long."

She was matter-of-fact, but Joel tried not to frown at the blanket pallet on the floor that apparently was going to serve as her bed. At least for now. He said nothing, though, knowing it might embarrass her.

Joel jabbed a thumb behind him. "We're going to unload some of Brooke's things. The house is great, Anastasia."

"Thanks!"

Her relaxed expression stayed with Joel as he and Chess hauled in a futon, an old loveseat, Brooke's bed and dresser, and a small collection of boxes she'd packed over the previous week.

They'd also found an extra dresser. Joel and Chess carried the piece of furniture to Anastasia's room. When she peered up from her spot on the floor, she stood quickly. "What's this?"

Chess brushed the dust off the top with one hand. "No one was using it and we thought you might be able to."

"It's been in the garage for years," Joel added, raising his eyebrow, daring her to argue with them.

Anastasia hesitated and Chess seemed to catch on that something was going on between them. He glanced curiously at Joel.

"Thank you." Anastasia motioned to the section of wall under the window. "If you'll put it right there, that would be awesome. It's kind of you both."

Joel went out to the truck and retrieved a plastic bin with a lid on it. He carried it back to Anastasia's room.

She was already taking clothing out of her rolling suitcase and putting it in the dresser drawers. When she saw him, her eyes went to the bin then to his face.

He set it down in one corner of the room. "I put together a few things for you yesterday. I thought you could use them." When she started to object, he held up his hand to stop her. "Take them, Anastasia. Don't make a big deal out of it. Okay?"

She smiled. "Thank you, Joel."

"You're welcome. We brought in a futon as well as a loveseat. I'm sure Brooke wouldn't mind if we moved the futon in here until you got a bed."

"No, I'll be fine. I'm planning on picking up a mattress after my next paycheck." She must have seen him open his mouth to speak because she gave him a stern glare. "Which is only next week. I think I'll live."

Joel chuckled. Yes, he was going to offer to give her an advance just this once. He admired that she would refuse to accept it. Even sleeping on a pallet on the floor was a huge upgrade from the van. "You're something else, girl."

He tried to swallow past a lump in his throat, working up the courage to voice his question. "If I brought fried chicken, potato salad, and drinks by Monterrey Park — say, around noon tomorrow — would I be able to persuade you and Epic to have a picnic lunch with me?"

A healthy dose of pink colored Anastasia's cheeks and she ducked her chin as a smile lit up her face. "Are you asking me out?"

"Well, you and Epic. We could make it a double

date, but I'm afraid I don't know many single dogs right now."

Anastasia's laughter was like music to Joel. He gently put a finger under her chin and brought her eyes to his. "Is that a yes?"

"It is."

"Good." He leaned forward, his lips brushing the skin near her ear. "I'm looking forward to it." He straightened when he heard someone walk past behind them and spoke unnecessarily loud. "I'd better go and help Brooke bring the last of her things in. That lady is a slave driver."

"Whatever!" Brooke's voice floated down the hall followed by chuckles all around.

Anna followed Brooke and Joel into the living room. While still sparsely decorated, it was a whole lot homier with the furniture in it. The room didn't echo now like it had when she'd first walked in.

She was curious about what Joel had put in that bin. But she'd decided to wait until they left to check it out.

Chess set a box down on the floor against a wall and then surveyed the room. "That's the last of it. Are you sure you'll be okay here?"

"We're going to be fine." Brooke flopped onto the futon. "Any idea what you guys are going to do with my room?"

Joel and Chess exchanged a look and it was Joel who answered the question. "Not yet. We're not in a hurry." He draped an arm around Brooke's shoulders. "You're going to be missed. I hope you realize that."

Brooke's eyes grew misty as she nodded. "I know. I'll miss you guys, too."

Anna watched the exchange between them and wondered what it'd be like to have such a strong support system.

Joel's eyes shifted to her face and she was afraid her thoughts might have been plastered there for all the world to see.

"I'd better get back to work." Chess gave Brooke a hug, his jaw set. "Congratulations on the new place." His voice was tense

"Thanks, Chess. I appreciate the help."

"Of course. Bye, Anna. Congratulations to you, too."

Anna thanked him and gave him a friendly wave.

Joel hugged Brooke, too, and then smiled at Anna. "Glad we could help out. I'll go and let you two get settled. My manager called in sick. I need to swing back by the diner and make sure my back-up is doing okay. Call if you ladies need anything. And I'll see you tomorrow at the park, Anastasia."

"I'll be there."

Anna thought the house seemed strangely quiet after the guys left. "Well, here we are."

Brooke put her hands on her hips and surveyed the area. "Here we are." She focused a watery gaze on Anna. "I feel as though I've moved away from home for the first time. It's weird."

Anna sympathized. "You guys are family. And whether you live there or here, that'll never change."

She helped Brooke with a few things, let Epic into the house, and then went into her new room. Sunlight came through the cracks in the white mini blinds, making the room bright and cheerful. After carrying the bin Joel had given her to the pallet on the floor, she sat crossed legged on the blankets.

Anna had no idea what to expect from the contents. She pulled them out one-by-one. Three packages of plastic hangers. Between those and the dresser, she'd have a place to put the few articles of clothing she owned. There were several toys for Epic, a soap dispenser, toothbrush holder, and a wastebasket.

But what brought the biggest smile to her face was the box of blueberry muffins from the coffee shop. A piece of paper was folded and taped to the top of it.

Anna carefully removed it, her eyes taking in Joel's handwriting.

Anastasia,

I'm excited for you and this new phase of your life. I'm proud of your determination that has led you to this point. Your ability to live in the moment and do what's necessary is something I find both endearing and inspiring.

Joel

Anna read the note again, warmth spiraling through her.

For the first time in weeks, she felt safe.

The moment his phone rang, Liam swiped the

screen. "Rick, you'd better have something for me, or I swear I'll strangle the life out of you." He resisted the urge to crush his phone in his hand and throw it to the ground.

"A real estate company ran Anna's social security number for a credit check. I can't tell you whether she's obtained a house through them. But I can tell you where the real estate office is located."

Finally! "Spit it out, man."

Rick gave him the name and address of the office. When Liam hung up, he opened the road map of Texas.

Quintin. It was less than an hour away.

His lips stretched wide as he said, in a sing-song voice, "I'm gonna find you."

Chapter Fifteen

Anna was in Monterrey Park with Epic, waiting for Joel to arrive. She found a picnic table that had a good view of the parking lot. She sat there and watched Epic explore the nearby grass. The sun was warm and while she still needed a long-sleeved shirt, no jacket was necessary.

She hoped the large number of birds, butterflies, and wildflowers meant nice weather might be here to stay.

Anna heard the popping of tires rolling over rocks in the parking lot. She rotated and noticed Joel driving towards her. "Come here, Epic."

The dog jogged to her side, his eyes intent on the new vehicle. She stood and clicked the leash to his collar.

He parked the vehicle and approached them with a wave. "How are you two on this beautiful Sunday?"

"We're good. How about you?"

"I slept a lot better last night knowing you were safe. And Epic, too, of course." He winked. Good grief, did his smile have to send her heart racing like this? "You two were comfortable in the house, then?"

Anna chuckled. "Oh, yeah. I took a shower without a time limit, I got to sleep without dog hair in my mouth, and I woke up warm. I'd say it was downright luxurious."

Joel laughed. "I'm glad."

"Thank you for your help with the move. And for the box. You thought of everything."

"You're welcome. For what it's worth, I may not know what's happened in your past. But in the end, it brought you here to Quintin. And I'm thankful for that." He held her gaze for a few breaths then pointed a thumb behind him. "I'll go grab the food if you're ready to eat. I don't know about you, but I'm starving."

"Sounds great. I'm pretty hungry, too." Anna had been anticipating this meal since Joel suggested it. Even more, though, she'd been looking forward to the company.

Joel carried a small plastic tub to the picnic table and set it on the ground. He pulled a vinyl tablecloth out. "Never hurts to set the stage."

Anna helped him drape it over the table. They then proceeded to unpack a container of fried chicken that was still warm, potato salad, macaroni salad, coleslaw, and rolls. When everything was all on the table, she placed her hands on her hips and surveyed the spread. "Wow, you outdid yourself."

Epic stood as close to the table as possible without touching it. He did nothing but stare at the food, his pink tongue licking his chops on occasion.

Joel patted the dog on the head. "I think he's hoping the chicken will get up and dance right off the table and into his mouth."

Anna got a length of rope out of the van and tied it to both a tree and Epic's leash. That way, he'd have a lot of space to wander around while they ate. Even after Anna got him set up, Epic still watched them with envy.

If previous meals were any indication, Anna suspected Joel would toss him scraps when they were done eating.

For now, her mouth watered at the thought of that fried chicken. She took a seat on one of the long benches, noting that Joel chose to sit beside her. "Everything smells amazing."

"I didn't know if you were a potato or macaroni salad fan so I brought both." He handed her a thick paper plate. "Dig in."

"Thank you. And I actually like both."

He smiled at her, his gaze lingering on her face for a handful of moments. "Me, too."

They got their food and began to eat.

Joel wiped greasy fingers on a paper towel. "I've only driven by this park before. It seems like a nice one."

Conversation flowed easily as they enjoyed their meal. To Epic's delight, Joel had several chunks of chicken for him along with a leftover roll.

After cleaning everything up, they decided to take a stroll through the park. Anna retrieved Epic's ball from the van before they started out. Joel held his hand out for it and she gave it to him.

He lobbed the ball and Epic didn't hesitate to

bound after it. The dog brought it back and Joel repeated the motion. The next time, Joel handed the ball to Anna.

She laughed. "I think he'd rather you threw it."

"Why's that?"

"You know the expression, 'You throw like a girl?' Yeah, I make that girl look good."

He raised an eyebrow at her. "Surely you exaggerate."

He was daring her. She brought her arm back as far as she could and threw the tennis ball with all her might.

Epic didn't have to run far before scooping it up off the ground not far from them.

"Wow." Joel shook his head in mock pity. "That was terrible."

"Told you." Epic brought the ball back and dropped it at Joel's feet. "See, even he knows it."

Ten minutes later, Anna pocketed the tennis ball. "That's all, boy. Come on, let's walk some more."

Epic meandered his way along the path while Anna and Joel walked side by side. Joel's arm brushed against Anna's, and each time, it completely distracted her.

They'd been strolling in comfortable silence for a while. When Joel spoke, his voice almost startled Anna. "May I ask you something?"

"Sure."

"When you moved here, where did you come from?"

Anna hesitated. She hadn't meant to, but Joel picked up on it immediately. What she didn't expect was for him to reach over and take her hand in his.

"What are you running from, Anastasia?"

Her mind scattered in all directions. What was she supposed to say? She wasn't ready to tell him what she was coming from — she might not ever be. Panic welled in her chest and she forced herself to focus on the pressure of his hand on hers. On the way he was lacing their fingers together and then giving a reassuring squeeze.

Mustering every bit of strength she had, she prayed she'd sound casual and said, "Epic and I came here from Utah."

"Wow, that's quite a ways. Did Epic ride in the passenger seat the whole time?"

Anna chuckled at that and cast him a sideways look.

"Every last mile."

Epic heard his name and had trotted back over to them. Anna ran her hand over his warm head.

"What made you stop in Quintin?"

She considered her answer. "I can't explain it except to say that, from the moment we crossed into town, I felt God was telling me to stop." She peeked at him from beneath lowered lashes. "Does that sound insane?"

"No, it doesn't." He stopped and moved to stand in front of her, their hands still linked. "It's always both humbling, and a relief, when God shows us that he has a plan and is going to help us achieve it."

Anna couldn't agree more. Coming to Quintin had certainly been an answer to prayer in more than one way. Now that she had this rental with Brooke, could she hope for some semblance of a normal life? Did she even know what that was?

Joel reached his other hand out and traced the outline of her jaw with a single finger. "I, for one, am grateful you stopped in Quintin instead of driving right through."

His eyes were intense as he studied her. He curled the same finger under her chin and gently tipped it up. A breath later, he dipped and softly touched his lips to hers. It was the briefest of kisses before he pulled away, his breath warm on her cheek. Then he claimed her lips again, gentle, yet confident.

Anna's heart beat wildly as if trying to escape the confines of her chest. What if things stayed like this? What if she actually found someone to share her life with?

But could she open herself up to him? Tell him about Liam and what had happened? She didn't think so. Not now.

Joel must have sensed the change because his lips left hers, hovering mere inches away. "Anastasia?" His gaze contained a mix of concern and confusion.

He deserved answers. He deserved an explanation. And she couldn't give him one right now. Joel must have seen that in her face because he released a frustrated breath of air.

"Joel, I…" Ugh, she hated this! Everything about it. Would she ever be able to outrun Liam's reach? The thought alone brought tears to her eyes. She refused to let them fall. "There are things in my past I can't talk about. Things I wish I could forget."

"There are things like that for all of us. I've got my share of memories I'd rather not ever speak about. As much because I'll have to relive them as anything. It's part of life." Joel reached out and touched her shoulder gently.

"I know." *Please help him understand.* "But this is

different. I don't know that I'll ever be able to tell you. Mine aren't just memories. I'll always wonder if they'll catch up with me. And if they do, I think your opinions of me would change." She took a step back away from him. "Please, Joel. You deserve someone who's honest with you and I can't do that right now."

The pain in his eyes bruised her heart. But there was nothing else to be done. He had no idea how much she wished things were different. The kiss had been incredible. Being held in his arms again sounded like heaven right now. But she didn't deserve it. Didn't dare risk her heart — or his.

"I understand that you're not ready to talk about things. I get it. But I want to make one thing clear." He put a finger on her chin. "I'll be here when you are. I'm here if you need me and I hope you'll give me the chance to prove you wrong. To show you that my opinion of you won't change."

"Thank you." Her voice was a whisper and tears threatened mutiny.

Joel held a hand out to her and she took it. "Let's walk for a while."

It was only after she got back to the house and safely in her room that she brought down her defenses and allowed the tears to escape. It was the first time she'd truly broken down and cried since leaving Utah. Maybe this was exactly what she needed.

Liam was certain he'd driven up and down every road in Quintin. A slight exaggeration, perhaps, but he was already tired of the small town. He was beginning to wonder if he might never find Anna.

He stopped at a red light. He was going through options when a van matching the description he'd been given passed in front of him.

Adrenaline surged. "Come on! Move!" He slammed the palm of his hand against the steering wheel. The light turned green and the car in front of him rolled slowly into the intersection.

Liam made a hard right, eyes searching for a hint of the green van. There. It turned left up ahead.

Careful to keep his distance, he turned to follow it.

Several blocks down, the van pulled into a driveway.

Liam steered his car close enough to be certain it was Anna getting out of the vehicle and going into the house. Apparently she still had that mangy mutt with her. Another car waited in the driveway.

She didn't live there alone.

A sneer pulled at the corners of his mouth.

"I found you."

The temptation to storm in there tonight and pull her out by her hair was almost too much. But after searching for her for this long…

Well, he had every intention of making her pay, first.

He wrote the address down and went in search of a hotel before his car was recognized.

Chapter Sixteen

Ever since leaving Anastasia at the park and coming home, Joel had been completely distracted. Now he was in the kitchen, pulling the full trash can out from under the sink and taking the bag to the dumpster in the alley behind the house. While his hands worked, his mind was busy imagining what might have happened to her in Utah.

What was bad enough that she didn't feel comfortable telling him about it? Different options went through his mind but none of them seemed realistic. Others left a bad taste in his mouth.

There were two things Joel was certain of.

One was that, while he held her in his arms, everything about it felt right. As if she belonged there. And when they'd kissed... It was going to be a long, long time before her sweetness faded.

But he also believed he had to leave all of this in God's hands. He'd pray for Anastasia. He'd pray for what might be a beginning to a relationship between them. But he couldn't — and wouldn't — push her to reveal more about herself than she was comfortable with.

Joel had to work to get the bag into the dumpster. He brushed his hands off on his pants and headed back to the house.

Anastasia needed a friend. She needed people in her life that cared. And he planned to be one of those people.

Whatever happened in her past, and however long it took for her to tell him, it would be worth the wait. Anastasia would be worth it.

When he got back inside, Chess was waiting for him. "I thought you'd gotten lost out there for a minute."

Joel shot him a withering glare. "I was a little preoccupied."

"How'd your date with Anna go?"

Joel was half surprised at the question then realized it was Chess's way of guessing what — or who — he was actually preoccupied with. "It was good." He must not have been convincing because Chess raised an eyebrow at him. "When I think I'm getting closer to her, she pulls away a little. She's afraid if I know what happened to her in the past, it'll change what I think about her now."

"Isn't that true for all of us, though?" Chess leaned against a wall. "We all have events in our past that threaten to choke out our future if we let them. The further away we get from those memories, the easier it is. It'll be that way for Anna, too."

Joel sighed. "I know you're right. But it's hard to stand by and watch her struggle when I'd much rather help." He shrugged. "But what can I do?"

"Not a thing."

Joel looked at Chess. "What have you been up to today?"

"Brooke called earlier and invited us over for dinner and a movie tonight. I wanted to get something for her. A housewarming kind of gift." Chess swallowed and shrugged. "I don't like losing people."

"You're not losing her, Chess. Neither of us are." But Joel knew it felt like that for Chess because Brooke wasn't here where Chess could keep her safe. "Things change, whether we want them to or not. What did you get?"

"A rose bush. I thought I'd plant it for her in the front yard somewhere. She's always liked roses."

Joel smiled. Brooke would be touched by the gesture. "I'm sure she'll love it. What time are we supposed to be over there?"

"Five."

Joel went about putting in a new trash can liner, his thoughts still lingering on Anastasia.

"Are you sure you don't mind that I invited the guys over tonight?" It was the second time Brooke had voiced the question.

Anna had already assured her that it was okay. But apparently she hadn't been convincing. At this point, though, it was ten minutes until five and a little too late to change their minds. "It's fine. We didn't get to thank Joel and Chess for their help. This will be a good way to do that. Besides, they're your family. Of course they're welcome here anytime."

Brooke leaned against the kitchen counter. "I should've waited until after your date with Joel before doing so, though." Her eyes were full of concern.

"I'm fine. Joel and I are fine." Mostly. "Seriously, dinner and the movie will be fun."

Her roommate finally smiled. "I'm glad you suggested these cookies. They smell amazing. I never did have anyone to teach me how to bake. I had to teach myself how to cook for the most part."

"Joel mentioned you grew up in foster care."

"From the time I was seven. The first few years were pretty rough. But I ended up with the Zieglers. And you couldn't ask for a much better placement than that short of adoption. I was able to stay there until I aged out of the system."

"I'm glad you found them. Joel speaks highly of them as well."

"Yes. I'd been there for several years when Joel came in. He'd been bounced around quite a bit. I remember he wouldn't speak to anyone. It took me a while to get him to talk to me. But I'm a bit persuasive." Brooke winked.

There was no denying that. Anna laughed. "What happened after that?"

"The two of us stuck together. I aged out of the system first by eight months. Our foster parents were actually nice folks and let me stay until Joel aged out, too. Then we set out on our own." She took on a faraway expression. "It was hard until we met Chess. He made our rag-tag group into a family." Brooke smiled. "We still exchange Christmas cards with the Zieglers. They have a houseful of teenagers now." She paused. "Joel mentioned you'd been on your own for a while. I know what that's like. If it weren't for the guys... Well, let's say I'm glad God created a family for me. We all need someone else we can count on." She eyed Anna. "Joel's a great guy, you know."

"Yeah, I know." He was one of the kindest, most thoughtful men she'd ever met. Just thinking about Joel made her heart flutter. If only she didn't have to worry about Liam...

But Liam was in her past — her life — whether she wanted him to be or not.

The doorbell chimed, startling both of them. They laughed and walked to the front door. Brooke opened the door and ushered the guys inside.

Joel sniffed the air. "Something smells amazing."

Brooke nudged Anna with her elbow. "We're baking cookies. I'm planning on making popcorn before the movie, too."

Chess cleared his throat. "Brooke, I brought something for you. Will you come out front for a minute?"

The timer on the oven went off.

Joel pointed towards the kitchen. "I'll help Anastasia finish up the cookies. Go ahead."

Brooke followed Chess outside.

Anna led the way back into the kitchen. She grabbed a pot holder and pulled the pan of hot cookies out of the oven before sliding another pan in.

Joel leaned in. "Double chocolate chip? Those look incredible."

Anna bit back a grin. She used the spatula to move the hot cookies to the counter. When she scooped up the last cookie, she held it out to Joel. "Want to taste-test and let me know if they pass inspection?"

"It would be a crime to pass up a warm cookie right out of the oven." He held his hand out and accepted the cookie. When he took a bite, his eyes closed. "Oh, these are amazing. But I'd better test more than one. It's important to have a large enough sample size before I make my final decision."

She planted her hands on her hips. "Tell you what. If you hand me that bowl of cookie dough, I'll turn my head when you reach for another one."

Joel's face lit up. "It's a deal." He got the bowl for her and consumed a second cookie in two bites. He reached for the cookbook still resting on the counter and carefully turned it over in his hands. The cover was scuffed and the book was filled to the brim with recipes. "Is this yours?"

Anna dropped the last of the cookie dough by rounded spoonfuls onto the cookie sheet and wiped her hands off on a towel. "It was Grandma's." She reached out and ran a finger down the spine. "She saved recipes her own grandmother shared with her. And they're all in that book. It's the only real thing I have from her. Other than the color of my eyes."

Joel smiled warmly and handed the book back to Anna. "I assume she's the one who taught you how to bake?"

"Yeah." Anna thought back to when she was a child standing on a stool to reach the counter. Grandma helped her cut melon into cubes for a fruit salad. "My grandparents raised me since I was two. Most of my favorite memories of her revolve around the kitchen."

"What about your grandfather?"

"He didn't set a toenail in the kitchen. Left that to us. But he'd eat anything we made." Anna laughed. The memories washed over her like warm sunlight. "These double chocolate chip cookies were his favorite." She bit her lip in an attempt to keep her emotions under control. Moments like this made her realize how much she missed them.

Maybe, now that she had a kitchen, she could bake regularly again. Especially since it made her feel closer to her grandparents.

"It's all worth it, you know."

Joel's words confused her.

"What do you mean?"

He took his pocket knife out and tapped it against his palm. "Losing the people we love is horrible. A nightmare. But of all the people I've lost, it was worth it. Because I wouldn't trade the good memories for anything."

Anna pictured her grandparents. They'd been amazing and incredibly patient with her. Heaven knew she had to have made things difficult for them at times. She even thought of Callie. They'd had a lot of fun together before everything changed at the end. "Yeah, it was. But that doesn't mean it's easy to let people in."

She was so afraid that Liam was going to show up again that she kept pushing Joel away. What if, two years from now, Liam had never shown up and then Joel was gone, too? How would she deal with that? The emptiness inside answered the question for her.

I sure wish you'd give me a hint of what my future

held, God. I'm stuck in limbo and I hate this.

She could hear Grandma's voice in her mind as clearly as if the woman had been standing there with her.

"Give it to God, Anna. He'll see you through."

❧ ♥ ☙

Anastasia's shoulders sagged and she kept her arms crossed in front of her as she stared at an invisible point on the wall.

Joel resisted the need to gather her close. "I think all of us who grew up without a strong family setting experience the same thing. When you're faced with a lot of loss, it's hard not to worry that you'll just encounter more of the same."

Epic walked in, his nose in the air. He didn't have to try to be at eye-level with the cookies. Anastasia wagged a finger in front of him. "Don't even think about it."

The timer went off. She pulled the pan of cookies out of the oven and slid the last one in.

Epic must've realized he wasn't getting a treat. He turned to Joel and greeted him with a wagging tail. "Hey, big dog. It's good to see you, too. I know, it's been such a long time." Joel scratched behind his ears. "You'd think he hadn't seen me in days."

"I'm sure it seems that way to him." Her eyes followed Epic as he sniffed around the kitchen then collapsed in front of the refrigerator, his chin on the linoleum. "I envy him, you know," she finally said, her gaze still on the dog. "I wish I could be that carefree. Go forward in life and not worry that the past was going to catch up with me, or that I was going to screw something up." Her voice wavered and she cleared her throat.

"It would be nice." Joel moved to stand next to her. "But when we dwell on the past, we let it crowd into the present. Fear gets control of our lives that way." He shrugged. "I think everyone deals with that to a degree. But those of us who lived such traumatic childhoods have a harder time letting it go and moving forward."

"Yeah." Her voice sounded thick with tears.

Joel's heart ached for her. He'd faced many of his own demons several years ago and sometimes the memories he'd pushed back still crept into his dreams. Chess and Brooke had been a big part in the healing process. Who did Anastasia have? *Lord, fill her heart with peace. I don't know what's happened to her in the past, but I pray you begin work in healing the wounds that continue to cause her pain. If there's any way I can help, please use me.*

Anastasia pushed hair back out of her face. "I'm learning to keep people at arm's length. I haven't always done that, you know. In a lot of ways, it's made things easier." She lifted her chin and peeked at him from beneath her lashes. "But it also scares me. I'm not sure where to draw the line. I don't want to be one of those women who wakes up at fifty completely alone." She shifted slightly and leaned against his side.

Joel gently tugged her to him, engulfing her in his arms. A sigh escaped her and he laid his cheek against her silky hair. "You aren't alone. You don't have to be." She tilted her head back to glimpse his face. "You have all of us. You have me." He touched her chin with his thumb and placed a whisper of a kiss to her forehead. "I understand that instinct to hold back and protect yourself. It's only natural. But it's not something you have to do with me. Or the rest of the gang." They heard the front door open and Joel dropped his hand from her chin to her shoulder. "You okay?"

"Better." Anastasia stepped away from him and took in a breath. "You seem to have that effect on me. You know, when you're not making me mad." Her watery eyes twinkled.

Chapter Seventeen

Liam held the binoculars to his eyes and watched as two men entered the house Anna appeared to be living in.

She'd found herself some kind of pack to take her in. Boy, she must've laid a real sob story at their feet. Pathetic.

She couldn't have known these people for long.

Jealousy and anger coursed through Liam's veins.

Once the front door closed again, he tossed the binoculars onto the passenger seat. They sank into the food wrappers and disappeared.

He was sorely tempted to break into the house tonight and solve his problems. Anna had his thumb drive somewhere and he had every intention of retrieving it.

But she'd made his life miserable the last few weeks. And he'd find a way to pay her back for that first.

Ideas lined themselves up in his mind.

Yes, he'd watch her for a day or two and then

he'd make sure she regretted turning her back on him.

❦

They ate pizza in the kitchen then moved to the living room for the movie.

Between the futon and the loveseat, there was plenty of room for everyone to sit. Brooke insisted that Anna and Joel take the smaller of the two pieces of furniture. Anna tossed her a warning glance and Brooke only winked.

As they settled in for the movie, Anna noticed Epic lying in the space between the kitchen and living room, eyeing everyone as they got settled. He discovered a new love for popcorn when Brooke was making it and now he was obsessed. Anna suppressed a chuckle.

Joel sat next to Anna. It was not lost on her that he grabbed a stack of four cookies and brought them out along with the popcorn. He liked her cookies. The thought made her happy.

The movie began to the sound of popcorn being munched all around the room. Anna had added extra butter to hers and didn't regret it one bit. She usually tried to limit how much butter or salt she consumed. But popcorn was her one vice. If she was going to eat it, it might as well be greasy and salty. Otherwise, what was the point?

The first few times she reached for a kernel and popped it into her mouth, Epic's head raised off the floor slightly. Five minutes later, he was snoozing. Apparently he'd decided to give up.

Anna had been looking forward to this particular

movie for a while. The plot had her attention from the beginning, yet it was also difficult to ignore Joel's presence. She found herself aware of everything he did, and it was driving her crazy. From the slight brush of his knee against hers to incredibly tempting curls at the nape of his neck.

She kept her hands clasped or made sure she was holding something. The last thing she needed to do was embarrass herself because she couldn't help but reach out and touch his hair. Good grief.

About halfway through the movie, Brooke paused it to give everyone a quick break. Popcorn bowls were returned to the kitchen, some people got something else to drink. Mostly everyone needed to stretch their legs.

Anna threw several pieces of popcorn to Epic, who caught them mid-air.

"I imagine that's what a great white looks like when it's jumping to swallow its prey." Chess held up a piece. "May I?"

"Sure." Anna watched with a giggle when the popcorn disappeared in Epic's maw and Chess shook his head.

"I wouldn't want to make that dog mad at me."

"No, you wouldn't," Anna confirmed, giving her dog a scratch behind the ear.

"Is everyone ready to finish the movie?"

They all got situated again. Out of nowhere, Brooke produced boxes of licorice. She handed one to Anna and then threw another to Chess before sitting down again.

"How can you possibly be hungry?" Anna asked her.

Joel shook his head. "The woman's never too full

for candy."

Brooke nailed him with a glare. "Oh hush." She motioned around her as the sounds of the boxes being opened filled the air. "I don't hear anyone complaining about the candy. Watch the movie, mister."

Joel's eyes twinkled with amusement. Anna giggled.

Anna hadn't had red licorice in forever. She reached for a piece and took a bite. The candy was fresh and fell apart in her mouth. Even better than she remembered.

A moment later, she reached for another, her eyes on the television. Joel must have had the same thought because her hand bumped his. She started to jerk away and stopped, holding her breath. She barely identified the outline of their hands against the darkness of the couch. They were a breath away from touching. Joel moved a single finger and lightly ran it down the palm of her hand until it lay across the tips of her fingers. Anna's heart raced in her chest.

Instinctively, she curled her fingers around his. As soon as she did that, he moved his hand until their fingers were laced and their palms were together. Joel squeezed her hand gently and continued to hold it in his own.

Ever since their walk in the park and their first — and only — kiss, Anna had missed this. His hand was much larger than hers and yet he held it with such gentleness. Several times, throughout the rest of the movie, he would lightly caress the top of her thumb with his own.

When the credits rolled, he placed a tiny kiss to

her wrist and released her hand. His eyes caught hers briefly and she gave him a shy smile.

The guys debated the fight scenes while Anna helped Brooke clean up. She'd noticed her new roommate couldn't stand for there to be any dishes in the sink when they went to bed. Truthfully, Anna preferred the cleanliness as well. So far, they'd gotten along wonderfully.

"I'd say the evening was a huge success," she told Brooke as they worked together to wash the last of the dishes.

"Me, too." Brooke glanced behind her as the guys continued to talk. "Moving out is going to be good for me. In a lot of ways. And I think it'll improve my relationship with the others, too. I needed space." Brooke lowered her voice. "You and Joel — you make a great couple, you know."

Anna focused on wiping off the kitchen counters and Brooke only chuckled.

They finished with the kitchen and Anna let Epic out for the last time of the night. It was a bit cool. She closed the door and watched him through the window. She noticed Joel's reflection in the glass as he stepped up behind her.

"Tonight was a lot of fun. Thanks for putting up with us."

Anna smiled. "Are you kidding? This was a blast. We may have to do this regularly."

"I'd like that." Joel nodded towards Chess. "I think we're going to head out. I hope you have a great day off tomorrow."

"Thanks. You, too." She thought he might move to kiss her, but he didn't. She followed him and told Chess goodbye then watched as the two men left.

A half hour later, Anna was lying on her pallet of blankets, her eyes on the dresser and the box of muffins on top of it. It was going to seem odd not seeing Joel tomorrow.

Before she lost her nerve, she picked up her phone and sent Joel a text.

❧ ♥ ❧

Joel hadn't been able to stop grinning since they left Brooke and Anastasia's house. Chess had teased him once or twice and he'd shrugged it off. He didn't care. Anastasia was finally relaxing around him and he enjoyed every minute of it.

It'd taken about all of his strength to not kiss her goodbye. But it would have been in front of the others and the last thing he wanted to do was make her uncomfortable. That was the reason he hadn't asked if he could see her tomorrow, too.

It was going to be a long rest of the weekend until Tuesday morning when she'd come in to work.

Joel frowned at that thought — the first time his smile had slipped. He'd gone to bed but wasn't able to fall asleep. The sound of a text message furrowed his brow. He reached over for his phone. When he read Anastasia's name on the screen, his heart raced.

I hope it's okay that I text you. Thanks again for the blueberry muffins. I'm trying to make them last. It's not working.

Joel grinned and immediately typed out his response.

Text me anytime. And you're welcome. Though don't feel like you have to make them last. I'll take you to the coffee shop and buy you more. Just say the word.

He watched the screen as if that might make a text appear sooner.

I'll remember that. A few moments passed. *Thanks for the movie. I had a lot of fun. I'm sorry I'm such a mess, though.*

Joel sat up in bed. He'd gone over their conversation multiple times through the day.

No reason to apologize. You're not a mess. You're beautiful.

He held his breath as he waited for her answer. A smiling emoticon appeared.

I'd probably better get off the phone. Epic's already snoring. You all wore him out.

Joel pictured Epic passed out on his back his snores filling the room. He laughed.

No worries. Sleep well, Anastasia.

Good night, Joel.

Joel turned the screen off and put his phone back on the nightstand.

"Thank you, Father. Help me to be mindful of what Anastasia needs. Help us both to move forward in your timing only."

With that prayer on his lips, he fell asleep.

Chapter Eighteen

Anna woke Tuesday morning with a smile on her face. The sun was shining, there was less of a chill in the air when she let Epic outside, and buds peppered the branches on most of the trees. Spring was her favorite season.

She and Joel had texted frequently yesterday and had decided to meet at the coffee shop before work today. Anna couldn't wait.

Since Brooke had left much earlier, Anna had the house to herself. She readied for work while Epic ate his breakfast. Then she made sure a large container of water was outside before putting him in the backyard for the day.

She watched him from the sliding glass door for a few moments. What if he realized how big he was and got over the fence? She doubted he'd do it. But she planned to come home at lunch to check on him the first week to make sure he was okay.

Ready to go, she shouldered her bag and stepped

outside. Right before she unlocked the van door, she noticed the tire nearest her was flat.

Anna groaned. "You've got to be kidding me." A sprint around the van revealed that the other tires had suffered the same fate. It couldn't be a coincidence.

Caution collided with fear. She ran to the front door, went back inside, and locked it behind her. All four tires — there's no way she'd driven over a field of nails. Someone did this.

Her mind immediately went to Liam. Surely not.

Suddenly, their rental home felt like a mansion. Goosebumps peppered her arms as she pulled out her cell phone and dialed Joel's number.

"Good morning, Anastasia. Everything okay?"

"Not really. Someone slashed my tires." She sank onto the futon. Her eyes flitted from one doorway into the room to another.

"I barely left my house. I'll come by and take a look. I'll give you a lift to work."

Anna leaned forward and rested one elbow on her knee. "Are you sure?"

"It's not a problem. I'll be right there."

He must have hung up then because the line went quiet. Anna didn't want him to go out of his way, but she sure felt better knowing he would be there soon. She watched for him through the window. When he pulled up in front of the house, she hastened to meet him.

Joel checked each of the tires and clenched his jaw. "It looks like someone used a knife. Probably bored kids or someone who gets a thrill out of causing trouble."

Anna only half heard what he said. All she could

focus on was how someone had a knife and specifically chose to use it on her vehicle.

It's not Liam. It can't be.

It was probably like Joel said and her van wasn't the only one targeted on the street.

She scanned the area behind her and shivered.

Liam leaned back in the seat of his car and watched as Anna and the man who came to her rescue drove away. The shock on her face when she'd seen the tires was priceless. That flash of fear was exactly what he wanted. He wanted her to be afraid of him. She should be *very* afraid.

He was torn between trying to get into the house and following them. He chose the latter and stayed some distance back to ensure Anna wouldn't spot him or his car.

Liam observed as they purchased four new tires and had them loaded into the back of the man's car. Then he followed them to J's Parkview Diner. Both of them disappeared inside.

Using his binoculars, he discovered that both appeared to work there. Interesting.

Joel was used to Anastasia walking Epic on her breaks. Her first one today was halfway through before he realized she was sitting outside on the curb. She'd been withdrawn and almost sad since he picked her up at the house that morning. He didn't blame her for being upset about her tires. She'd finally agreed to let him pay for them with the promise that she'd pay him back.

The first opportunity Joel had, he went to join her outside. "Is this spot taken?" When she shook her head, he sank down beside her. "You seem lost in thought. Are you worried about Epic?"

"Some. I don't think he knows he could get over that six-foot fence if he wanted to. But I'd feel better knowing he's still in the backyard where he's supposed to be." Anastasia hesitated. "The tire thing bothers me."

"I'm sorry this happened to you. I'll arrange to take my lunch at the same time that you do and we'll go check on Epic. Chess said he was coming by your house tonight to install the motion light. We'll put the new tires on then. How does that sound?"

She agreed and smiled at him. "That'll be great. You guys are awesome."

Her smile was short-lived, though.

Joel put a hand on her arm. "What else is bothering you?"

She shrugged. He didn't think she was going to say anything until she tilted her head to see him. She massaged her temples before twirling a section of hair around one finger. "Back in Utah, I was involved with someone. He was my boss and that worked for a long time before we started going out."

Anastasia hesitated and Joel waited patiently for her to continue.

"He was obsessive and controlling. Scary. When I broke it off, he wasn't happy. I knew that I wouldn't be able to relax if I stayed there."

"You thought he was going to hurt you."

Anastasia nodded.

Joel's blood boiled. He clenched a fist to keep from saying more than he ought to right now. "You did the right thing by leaving."

"I didn't have much of a choice given the circumstance."

Joel was convinced she wasn't telling him everything. He wanted to know more, but had to be content with this for now. That she was opening up to him at all was a big thing.

She released a slow breath. "When I saw those tires this morning, I freaked out. What if he followed me all the way here?"

"Do you think he'd track you halfway across the country?" Something flashed in Anastasia's eyes. She did. What on earth happened back in Utah? "More than likely, it was a couple of punk kids who had nothing else to do but slash a bunch of tires. I'm sure I'd be worried, too, in your position. But hopefully it was something random and has nothing to do with that guy."

"Sure." She didn't look convinced. She leaned over and let her head rest against his arm.

Joel breathed in her scent and they sat in silence for a few minutes. His mind kept replaying what she told him. No wonder she'd been hesitant about opening up to him. "I need you to know I'd never try to control you. My biggest wish for you is that you feel safe and happy."

She put her arm around his and squeezed. "I know. You're nothing like him."

He placed a kiss against her hair. He may not know much about the guy from her past, but he couldn't imagine anyone wanting to cause her pain.

The door opened and Adam stuck his head out.

"You've got a call, boss."

Joel stood and reached a hand down to help Anastasia to her feet.

That evening, Anna and Brooke sat on the small front porch and watched as Joel changed the tires on Anna's van. Meanwhile, Chess was working to install a motion light on the side of the house facing the driveway.

The temperature had warmed considerably since last week and a gentle breeze carried the scent of freshly-mowed grass.

Anna expected to regret telling Joel as much as she had about Liam. Instead, there was relief.

For a long time, she'd had no one she could rely on.

And now… Now she had three friends who went out of their way to help. And Joel. What exactly was Joel? Her boss? Friend? No, he was more than that.

He made her heart race like no one else ever had. When she wasn't around him, she couldn't stop thinking about him. And when he smiled at her…

Anna swore the temperature rose ten degrees.

Joel picked the last tire up off the pavement and carried it to the van. By the time he had it on and the jack put away, Chess had finished his work as well.

Joel rolled the flat tire near the others. "These things are practically vintage." He turned to Anna. "You're probably lucky they didn't split on you before this happened. Whoever slashed those tires may have done you a favor."

Yeah, Anna didn't know about that. But she

probably was fortunate to have made it all the way from Utah without having a blowout.

Chess brushed his hands off on his pants. "Well, hopefully the motion sensor will pick up anyone who comes sneaking around at night again." He turned his gaze to Brooke. "If you guys have any trouble tonight, call us."

"Yes, sir." Brooke's voice was sarcastic, but her eyes said otherwise. She smiled at Chess, stood, and gave him a hug. "Thanks."

"Anytime."

When Brooke stepped back again, she ambled to the corner of the porch. She reached out to touch a leaf from the rose bush Chess had planted for her.

Anna stood, too. "Yes, thank you." Joel joined them on the porch. "And a big thank you for changing the tires. I appreciate your help."

"All in a day's work." Joel gave her a smile. He moved to stand next to Anna. "It's been a long day, hasn't it?"

"It sure has." Anna yawned and covered her mouth with a hand. "Sorry."

Joel checked the time on his phone. "Don't worry about it. We should probably get going and let you girls get some rest."

Chess went to toss an old tire into the back of his truck. "I'll get rid of these for you tomorrow."

Joel helped Chess load the rest. When finished, Joel pulled Anna aside.

"You mentioned you wanted to get some things after getting your paycheck today. I thought maybe we could go together tomorrow. What do you think?"

"I'd like that. What about the mall? I heard there

was a container store there I'd like to check out." Anna was already looking forward to spending the evening with him.

"Sounds great. How about I meet you here at your house tomorrow at six-thirty?"

"That'll be perfect." Anna smiled up at him.

Chess was waiting for him. He stepped forward and placed a kiss to her cheek. "I'll see you in the morning. Breakfast?"

"I'll be there."

He flashed her a grin before reaching for her hand and holding it as they joined the others. They received a happy smile from Brooke and Joel got an elbow jab from Chess.

Chapter Nineteen

Anastasia sat on the front porch the next evening waiting for Joel when he arrived at her house. She hopped up and jogged to the passenger seat. She wore a pair of dark jeans and a blouse that flowed down past her hips. He was used to seeing her in t-shirts. The more feminine choice was noticeable. He opened the door for her. "You look beautiful."

She smiled shyly and got into the car. He closed her door and went around to his own seat. "Ready to go?"

Anastasia nodded and he directed the car towards the mall. Fifteen minutes later, they stepped through the main entrance as other shoppers wandered in and out of stores.

"What are you shopping for today?" This particular mall was filled with outlet stores — everything from clothing to luggage.

"I want to check out that store here that has a lot of things for storage and organization. But we can

hit that one last in case what I decide to get is bulky."
She shrugged. "Otherwise, I thought we could
mostly wander a little. I need shorts. The weather's
warming up now and I don't have any."

"None?"

Anastasia's eyes widened as if she realized
something. "I...I didn't bother bringing them with
me when I moved here."

The last thing Joel wanted was for her to be
uncomfortable. He reached for her hand and gave it
a reassuring squeeze. "Shopping for shorts it is. I'm
mostly looking forward to spending time with you."

"I am, too. With you." She rolled her eyes. "Let's
go before I bury myself any deeper."

Joel laughed loudly.

A half hour later, they decided to split up so that
Anastasia could try on shorts. After agreeing to meet
back at the small fountain a few stores down from
the clothing store, they went their separate ways.

Joel spent his time browsing an Army surplus
store. When he approached the fountain, he spotted
Anastasia already there, her eyes on the moving
water. She hadn't seen him yet and he enjoyed
having a moment to admire the way her hair flowed
down her back, catching the light from the large
skylight in the ceiling above.

He sat down next to her. "Hello, stranger."

She smiled. "Hello."

He pointed to the bag at her feet. "Found some?"

"I did. Thank goodness. I'm not big on shopping,
especially when I need to find something that'll fit.
But yeah, I'm good to go."

Joel peeked at his phone. He wanted to take her
out for dinner, but it was already getting late. He

knew she wanted to go in at least one or two more stores. Hopefully mall food would be okay. "Do you want to check out the food court? You can get anything you want — I'm buying."

"Sure."

They walked hand-in-hand to the food court. They both decided on Chinese food and carried their heavy plates to a nearby table.

Anastasia blinked at all of the food. "I can't possibly eat all of this. There's enough for two people on each of these plates."

"Maybe next time we can just get one and share it." Joel watched as her lips curled upwards.

"That sounds like a good idea."

They mostly ate in silence as they watched groups of people file past. When they'd finished, he handed her a mint he'd grabbed off the counter and popped a second one into his mouth. He took their plates to the trash and then sat opposite her. Anna's eyes skimmed the crowd and stopped at him.

Joel reached across the table and covered her hand with his. "You have the most beautiful eyes I've ever seen."

His comment seemed to catch her off guard. Her eyes widened and she dropped her gaze to her hands. "Thank you." A small smile graced her lips.

Sensing she needed to be rescued, he stood. "Come on, let's get back to shopping."

He offered to carry the bag Anastasia held. Once ready, he weaved his fingers with hers and led her away from the fountain.

Every time the guy touched Anna, Liam's blood boil. Who did he think he was, anyway? And there she was, soaking it all in. She'd never looked at Liam the way she was gawking at the guy right now.

Which only irked him more.

He imagined his thumb drive in her pocket or nestled in the bottom of the small bag she was carrying.

Liam called that morning to find out whether the insurance company was going to pay for the fire damage done to his agency.

Apparently the investigation had been completed and the fire was declared an accident. The claim would be processed.

Which ought to make Liam happy. He should cut his losses and go home, collect the money, and move forward.

But if Anna ever found a way to gain access to those files...

And the thought of *her* living happily here with *him*...

No. He needed to tie up these loose ends. And soon.

This shopping trip turned into a relaxing evening for Anna. Spending time with Joel was enough to do that. But she'd also found most of the things on her list. Combine that with dinner and now walking hand-in-hand? She wasn't in a hurry to leave.

Joel tugged on her hand to stop their progress. "What's left?"

"Just the storage store. Unless you'd like to look

somewhere else."

Joel shook his head. "I don't think so. The storage store it is." He smiled brightly.

He took her hand in his and placed a kiss to her wrist.

She liked it when he did that. It was sweet.

They were nearing the storage store when a chill raced through Anna. At first, she thought it'd gotten cold until she realized the hair on the back of her neck was standing up. The impression that someone was watching her was strong enough that her feet stopped moving of their own accord.

"What's wrong?"

She heard Joel's words but didn't answer. Her eyes swept the area around them. Nothing unusual. And then...

Her breath rushed from her lungs as if someone had dropped a boulder on her chest.

There, several stores away, half-hidden by a pillar.

Liam.

He caught her eye and sneered.

She jumped, releasing Joel's hand along with the bag she'd been carrying.

Joel put a hand on her back. "What's going on?" His eyes darted from her to the pillar and he tensed.

When Anna checked again, there was no sign of the man that had plagued her nightmares since she'd left Utah.

Joel reached over and took her bag. "It was him, wasn't it?"

She jogged towards the storage store. "Yes. Come on, we have to leave."

"Anastasia..."

"Please, Joel. You don't understand what he's capable of. I'll explain everything to you. But we need to get out of here."

He took complete charge then. He grasped her hand and they ran to the container store, up and down several aisles, then out the door at the back that exited the building.

They were a block away from where Joel had parked the car. But she didn't care. She was relieved Joel stuck close to the mall and turned several corners, cutting off any view someone might have of them. Several times, she surveyed behind them and didn't see a sign of Liam.

How did he find her?

Did he know where she lived?

Joel led her through the maze of cars to his. He got her settled into the passenger seat, tossed the bags in the back, and climbed in. "Your house is closer. Let's go there."

She could only nod as she twisted in her seat to take in the parking lot. Still no sign. Hopefully Liam hadn't been able to get out fast enough to follow them. Her heart raced painfully.

Joel got out of the parking lot as quickly as he could and soon they were on the road. She kept her eyes on the console in front of her, willing herself to keep it together.

She'd thought Quintin would be safe. She thought Texas was far enough away. But if he found her here...

Anna had friends. Joel. She didn't want to leave again. But she couldn't put anyone else in danger. She should have kept moving and never stopped here in the first place. Her eyes filled with tears and she tried to blink them away.

Joel's hand touched her arm and she jolted. He shot her a worried glance. "You're shaking. Hang on, we're almost there."

They pulled into the driveway. Anna was out and on her way to the front door before Joel even had a chance to help her. She fumbled with her keys and barely inserted one into the lock when it opened from the inside. Brooke greeted them with a smile that fell away the moment she saw their faces.

"What's going on?"

Anna pushed her way inside and crossed her arms tightly across her chest. She was immediately met by Epic, who wriggled and whined at her feet. She absently fingered his ear and released a breath of relief as Joel closed and locked the door behind them.

She prayed they'd managed to escape before Liam had the chance to follow them.

Please, God. Please keep us hidden from him. I want this to be a bad dream and wake up again.

Joel stood in front her, a hand on each of her upper arms. "You're worrying me, Anastasia. What on earth is going on?"

Anna shook her head. What was she supposed to do now? She had to tell them. They had the right to know.

Chapter Twenty

Joel watched Anastasia. His stomach rolled while his mind raced through the possibilities. She was staring straight ahead, trembling. He'd only caught a glimpse of a man at the mall. But there was no missing the hatred in the guy's eyes. Joel took her hand and led her to the loveseat. "Sit down. I'm going to get you a glass of water."

"I'll get it," Brooke announced on her way to the kitchen.

Joel sat down next to Anastasia. Brooke returned. She placed a glass on a side table and pulled it over in front of Anastasia before sitting on the futon. Brooke's eyes were filled with questions.

Epic was lying across Anastasia's feet, his dark eyes watching her every movement.

Joel reached over and covered her hand with his. "Should I call the police?"

Anastasia shook her head.

Brooke caught Joel's eye and mouthed, "Text

Chess?"

Joel nodded and turned his attention back to Anastasia. "We can't help you if you don't tell us what's going on."

For the first time since they'd reached the house, her gaze shifted to his face. The connection seemed to calm her and her breathing slowed. "I never wanted to get you all involved. I thought I'd gone far enough."

"I care about you. That alone makes me involved." He raised an eyebrow and waited for her to process what he'd said.

She sank into the back of the futon and ran a hand over her face. "I saw a man named Liam Graff at the mall today. I left Utah because of him. I didn't think there was any way he'd trace me here." She shuddered.

Joel leaned into the corner of the loveseat where the arm met the back. He reached for her and brought her to him, her back resting against his chest. She let her head fall against his shoulder. He breathed in the scent of her hair and waited for her to continue.

After hesitating at first, she shared about her grandparents' death and how Liam had been instrumental in getting her off the streets. She told them about her friend Callie and the job at the advertising agency that Liam owned.

At first, Liam seemed like a nice guy who was trying to give people — kids — a chance to make something of themselves.

But when she related about how charming he'd been until they started going out and about how she couldn't go anywhere without Liam demanding a minute-by-minute account, Joel clenched his teeth together.

"I guess I knew I had to figure a way to get out of there when he cornered me in the supply room one day." Anastasia paused. "I'd spilled a whole ream of copy paper and that's when he came in. His face turned red and he yelled at me, telling me I was costing the company money when I was so careless." She shivered. "He shoved me against the wall and told me that every last piece of paper had better be usable or I'd be sorry. It was just paper."

Brooke gasped, a hand going to her mouth. Joel's arms tightened around Anastasia.

Rage boiled and he'd punch the guy out right then if he had the opportunity. Anastasia must have sensed it because she turned her head to the side and up in order to view his face. He kissed her forehead. "I have no respect for a man who tries to take advantage of someone like that. He clearly considers women to be beneath him."

If Joel thought he was upset now, it was nothing after he heard about how Liam had accused her of stealing money and that her friend, Callie, hadn't even stood by her side. Much less when Liam tried to blackmail her with it.

No wonder Anastasia hesitated to trust other people.

"Is that why you left?"

Anastasia shook her head. "No, things got worse." She snuggled further into his arms.

Worse? The muscles in Joel's shoulders tightened. He rubbed the top of Anastasia's arm.

A knock at the door sent Epic into a fit of barking. Brooke stood to answer it.

Joel spoke from his spot on the loveseat. "Make sure you know who's there before you unlock that door."

Brooke peeked through the hole in the door then opened it. The moment Epic recognized Chess, his tail wagged. He greeted the newcomer and then resumed his watch at Anastasia's feet.

Chess's eyes were on Brooke. "You said it was an emergency. What's going on? Are you okay?"

Anastasia explained what happened to them. Chess watched Anastasia, concern shifting to protectiveness and anger. Joel knew he'd understand in a heartbeat. Chess turned around and secured the door before he joined Brooke on the futon.

Joel kissed Anastasia's shoulder. "Tell us what happened next."

Anna focused on the safety of Joel's arms. She'd been afraid to tell him any of this and, to a degree, she still was. But finally sharing the burden of what she'd been carrying around for weeks was a relief.

Her mind drifted back to the catalyst. The final event that had led her to pack up her things and disappear. Anna took in a deep breath.

"I suspected Liam was taking money from the company. We lost our main account, but even then, the money was getting drained way too quickly. When he accused me of stealing some, I worried he was trying to blame me for all of it.

"One evening, Liam gave me a bunch of junk to do that kept me at the office late. I remember being angry about it, because it was all stuff that could be done the next day, but he'd insisted. Told me if I didn't stay, he'd fire me." She swallowed. Boy, she wished she'd simply told him no then. Everything else may not have happened. "I was sitting at my desk just outside of Liam's office. I remember it was almost ten because I'd just checked the clock. I was exhausted. All of a sudden, I smelled smoke as it came in from under the door to the supply room. The sprinkler system came on, a fire alarm sounded, and the building filled with smoke."

Joel drew her closer to him and Anna accepted the warmth and security his presence offered. She let her gaze roam over the faces of her friends. All of them were listening with rapt attention.

"I remember jumping up from my desk and looking over at the window. Something caught my eye. Outside, Liam was watching me..." Her voice caught. "It was like staring into the face of a monster. His eyes had no emotion in them but his mouth — no one smiles that wide naturally. I knew he set that fire. I have no idea if he was trying to kill me, or if he hoped I'd go down for setting it myself."

Chess cursed. His voice startled her, but he didn't say anything she hadn't already thought.

"What'd you do next, Anna?" The question came from Brooke.

"I don't know why I didn't get out of the building. But the moment I realized Liam was behind the fire, it was clear my life might depend on having proof. I knew where he kept all of his backups. I ran into his office first..."

"...and grabbed the thumb drive," Joel finished for her.

Anna's gaze rested on Epic and the cylinder dangling from his collar. She put a hand on her other arm. "I grabbed it, knowing that if he was stealing money from his own company, the proof would be on there. Then I ran for the back of the building and got out. He never saw me leave. I don't know if it was because of the fire department showing up or what, but I got the head start I needed."

What was Joel thinking? Did he wonder whether she was telling the truth?

Uncomfortable with the silence, Anna kept talking. "I withdrew all my money from the bank and paid cash for the van. I got rid of my phone and picked up the one I have now. Epic and I drove. For hours. Days. Until we got here. I was hoping I could use the files to incriminate Liam but then I couldn't decrypt them. I shouldn't have stopped here — I should have kept going."

And there it was. All out on the table for the others to judge. Did Joel regret giving her a job or introducing her to his family?

His voice rumbled near his ear. "I'm not sorry you stopped in Quintin."

Those words did more to soothe her soul than she ever thought possible. When the others echoed his sentiment, tears filled her eyes.

"I didn't think there was any way he'd find me here." Anna sat up and shifted so she could see him. "What if he knows where I live? Where you all live? I don't know what he's capable of." She shuddered. "I'm sorry for all of this. I need to pack up and move on before he finds me. I don't want to put any of you in danger."

"No." Joel's firm word drew her eyes to his. "If

he followed you here, he won't stop until he catches up with you. You didn't set that fire and there has to be a way to prove it. Let us help you."

Chess's booming voice filled the room. "Someone like that won't stop at hurting you. He'll keep finding ways to do that until he's put behind bars."

Anna blinked at him. At the rest of the people in the room. "You believe me?"

"Why wouldn't we?" Joel gently cradled her face with both of his hands. "I wish you'd told me about all of this before now. But I get that you were trying to protect us." He brushed his thumbs against her cheeks. "Do you want to leave Quintin?"

She immediately shook her head. "No."

"Good. You're not alone now."

Relief ran through her veins to every part of her body. "Thank you." Her voice was barely above a whisper.

Joel moved to stand and drew her up with him. "Regardless of whether he knows where you live, I'm not comfortable with you and Brooke staying here alone."

"I agree." Chess stood. "You two should come back to our place until this gets settled." He was watching Brooke as if he expected her to argue. But when she agreed, he appeared relieved.

Brooke looked at Epic. "What about the thumb drive?"

Chess eyed the dog. "If Liam wants it this badly, I'm willing to bet he's got the key needed to decrypt the files on him. The safest place for that drive is right where it's at now."

Epic raised his head as though he understood their every word.

Anna listened to the surrounding conversation. Joel believed her.

Thank you, God.

It felt like déjà vu as Anna took her clothing off their hangers and out of the drawers. She should've known these few days in paradise wouldn't last forever.

She hadn't realized how much force she was using to stuff the clothing into her rolling bag until Joel came up behind her. "Destroying your things isn't going to stop Liam." He put his arms around her and she stilled.

Sagging back against him, she welcomed the support of his sturdy chest and the warmth of his arms. "I hate him. And I hate myself for having been duped by him in the first place." She frowned, frustrated by the prickling of tears. She was sick of wanting to cry.

Joel brushed a kiss against her ear. "Come on, let me help." Together, they finished packing and met the others in the living room.

Anna spent the entire drive to Joel's house watching the surrounding vehicles. It was dark and difficult to pick out details, but that didn't stop her from holding her breath along the way. She half expected to find Liam waiting on the front porch.

Joel parked his car and they got out. Epic had ridden in the back seat, his ears bent and an annoyed expression on his face. But as soon as Joel let him into the house, he seemed to forgive them for banishing him from the passenger seat.

The others arrived. Chess and Joel insisted on going inside first. They came out a few minutes later.

"Everything's secure," Chess said. "It's possible he doesn't know where we live." He didn't seem convinced.

"I only wish I knew how he'd found me in the first place. I did everything I could think of to disappear."

"I don't know." Joel watched her carefully. "If his whole world was in that agency, he's probably had nothing else to do but track you down since it burned. This isn't simply about getting that disc from you. It's personal to him."

Liam had known the car she'd had before the van. He might've been able to locate it, find out that she paid cash for the van. But then what? Asked around at every gas station in existence to see if she'd stopped there? Obsession at its finest.

Surely there were times she'd been alone when Liam might have made a move. What was he waiting for?

Her stomach clenched. What would she have done if he had come after her? She shook off the thought, the consequences too terrifying to entertain.

Anna wasn't alone now.

Chapter Twenty-One

Chess had gone online and located a picture of Liam Graff. It wasn't difficult since the website for the advertising agency remained active.

Joel stared at the guy's face. He may not have gotten a good view of him in the mall, but there was no doubt this was the same person. Liam looked like a greasy car salesman. That the man had ever laid a hand on Anastasia... He clenched his fist.

All reports on the fire that destroyed the building said it was determined to be an accident. If the guy was getting his money, why didn't he just take it and run? Why was he so determined to come after her?

There were only two viable options, and both left his blood running cold.

Either Liam had found a way to frame Anastasia and intended on getting her back to Utah to pin it all on her. Or since she knew he started the fire, he wanted to make sure she didn't talk. Either way, if Liam managed to get hold of the thumb drive and shut Anastasia up, he'd likely get away with the whole thing.

"We can't sit around here waiting until the guy decides to move on or show his hand. But we shouldn't leave either of the girls alone just in case."

"Agreed." Chess printed two copies of Liam's photo. He handed one to Joel and kept the other for himself.

He was about to say something else when Brooke peeked her head out from the kitchen. "I'm pulling out sandwich fixings if anyone else is interested."

It was a mutual, silent decision to put off the discussion until later.

By the time eleven in the evening had arrived, they had everything worked out. Chess would take Brooke to work and bring her home again. Anastasia would go to work with Joel. Since Chess carried a concealed handgun, he planned to swing by the girls' house a couple times through the day to see if he could catch Liam watching it.

Chess and Joel worked together to get Brooke's old room set up for the girls.

Given the lateness of the hour and that the decisions had been made, Joel should have been able to sleep. But every time he closed his eyes, he pictured Anastasia's face when she'd first seen Liam at the mall. She'd been terrified. He wanted to protect her from experiencing anything like that again. At two in the morning, he gave up on sleep. He padded his way to the kitchen in search of a snack.

The house was quiet and everything seemed to be in order. He was surprised to find Anastasia sitting at the dining room table in the semi-darkness. She jumped slightly when she heard him and then smiled apologetically. "Sorry. I can't sleep. I hope I didn't wake you."

"No, I woke up all on my own. You have nothing to apologize for." He shrugged and noticed she had nothing in front of her. "Care for a cup of hot chocolate?"

"That would be great. Thank you."

"Sure. You go sit on the couch and relax. I'll be right back."

A few minutes later, he placed their mugs along with a sleeve of cookies on the coffee table. "They aren't nearly as good as yours, but they'll work in a pinch." He offered her a cookie.

She took it from him. "These are great."

They ate their snacks and whispered when they spoke. Mostly, they sat in comfortable silence.

Anastasia finished her second cookie and set her half-empty cup on the table.

Joel drained the last of his hot chocolate. He didn't miss the heaviness in her eyes. He settled against the back of the couch. "Come here, Anastasia."

She didn't hesitate to relax against him, her head resting on his shoulder. He put an arm around her to draw her closer. She snuggled into his side. Within moments, Anastasia's breathing became even. Joel leaned forward. Her eyes were closed and she was in a deep sleep. He pressed a kiss to her hair and laid his cheek against her head.

He wouldn't have had her move for the world.

The sun seeped through the curtains, waking Joel after what seemed like ten minutes of sleep. His arms stiff, he tried to stretch without disturbing Anastasia. She shifted slightly.

Joel checked his watch. It was shortly after six. The rest of the household would be up soon. "You awake?"

"Under protest." Her voice was a whisper.

Joel chuckled and used his hand to move the hair off of her face. "I hear ya."

She groaned as she sat up and stretched. "How much trouble would I be in if I admitted to my boss I don't want to go to work today?"

"A lot." He lifted an eyebrow at her. "I have to go in and you're coming with me. I'm not letting you out of my sight today."

<hr />

Liam hadn't anticipated the entire bunch of them to retreat to one house like they had. On one hand, he took great pride in the fact that he had four adults scared enough to do exactly that. On the other, having them together was going to make it a lot more difficult to draw Anna out.

He watched as Anna got into Joel's car and they drove away. He grabbed a notepad from the seat next to him. Chicken scratches covered the top sheet of paper, along with coffee stains and dried beans from one of his burritos.

Liam had made notes about everything. What time each of the members of the little pack left for work and returned, the fact that it was usually Brooke who checked the mail, and how the mutt stayed outside during the day but inside at night.

No detail was lost on Liam. And each was going to be equally important when it came time for him to make his move.

He was tired of hotels and spending most of his day in the car.

No matter what it took, this was ending. Tonight.

The only question was how much misery he could put Anna through between now and then.

With a chortle, he revved the engine and took off in the direction of the diner.

Joel secured the safe and scanned the dining area in time to see Anastasia sink into one of the booth seats and rest her head on her folded arms.

It'd been a long day. Both of them had been at the diner from opening until it closed. It was finally time to head back home and he was more than ready. From the look of things, Anastasia was, too.

He approached her quietly in case she'd fallen asleep. "Anastasia? You awake?"

She groaned and rolled her head from side to side on her arm.

Joel chuckled and slid onto the bench beside her. "Come on, girl. Don't make me carry you to the car." When she glimpsed his face to see if he was joking, he waggled his eyebrows at her. He more than enjoyed the blush that crept into her cheeks. "Sorry, I couldn't help it."

"Right." Anastasia rotated her shoulders and waited for him to move before standing herself. "I don't know how you work this many hours regularly."

Joel reached for her hand. "I admit it was a bit of a beating today. Let's turn off the lights and get out of here."

They'd barely done so when Anastasia paused. "Do you smell that?"

Instantly alert, Joel inhaled. The acrid smell was faint, but there was no mistaking it.

"Smoke," they said together.

Anastasia scanned the restaurant. "Where's it coming from?"

Joel let her into the back of the store where the smell was stronger. He grabbed the fire extinguisher off the wall and went to the back door of the diner. Upon opening it, smoke billowed towards them.

Through watering eyes, he realized the fire seemed to be contained in the metal dumpster at the end of the building. He closed the diner door behind him to keep as much smoke out of the place as possible.

Anastasia coughed. Joel positioned her against the wall as far from the fire as he could, but close enough to still keep an eye on her. "Stay here."

He pulled the pin from the fire extinguisher and battled the flames. The wooden fence that surrounded the dumpster on three sides was at risk of catching fire. If that happened, it was possible the flames could spread to the diner.

"Be careful, Joel!"

Joel squinted against the heat that tried to sear his skin. Sweat rolled down his back as he doused the last of the flames.

He turned to find Anastasia right where he'd left her. "Are you okay?"

She nodded, eyes wide. "Are you?"

"I'm fine." He tossed the fire extinguisher to the ground at his feet. He checked the area on either side of the diner. A hose attached to a faucet nearby served as a way to clean off the sidewalk. He used the water to drench the contents of the dumpster to ensure they wouldn't catch fire again.

The whole time, he kept his teeth clenched hard enough to make his jaw hurt. What kind of games was the guy playing at? What if the diner had caught fire? What if Anastasia had been hurt?

Joel coiled the hose up and then delivered a swift kick to the dumpster. He locked the diner. "Come on, let's get you to the car."

He put a protective arm around Anastasia's shoulder. He'd spent many years holding himself responsible for what happened to his parents, wondering if they'd have lived if he had been in the car instead of at school.

The last thing he wanted to see was anything happen to Anastasia or the rest of his family.

He realized he was beginning to think of her as part of his family. And he liked that a lot.

Joel placed a kiss to her temple and escorted her to the driver's side door.

She was the first to spot the piece of paper taped to the window.

You are delusional if you think these people are your friends, Anna. You're like a lost puppy that they've taken in and fed because they can't stand to see you sad and lonely. That's all you are to them. Trust me, I know. That's all you ever were to me, too. One day, they will kick you to the curb like you deserve. And you'll wish you'd never crossed me in the first place.

Joel read the note over Anastasia's shoulder. When he got to the bottom, he gently turned her around to face him.

"The very fact that he would write something this cruel and heartless tells you how untrue those words are. Don't you believe a word of it. You hear me?"

"I hear you." She handed the note to him. "He was never a good person, not even that first day I met him. I was too naïve to realize it at the time." She shook her head. "I almost feel sorry for him."

"I don't." Joel took the paper and resisted the urge to crumple the note or burn it. "Let's call the police and report this. The more evidence we have showing how unstable Liam is, the stronger your case against him will be."

Chapter Twenty-Two

Anna was silent all the way back to the house. Joel didn't speak, either. Which was fine. She doubted either of them could've come up with something to say right now.

She knew that the note Liam had left for her was nothing but lies. But it still hurt. Not because she doubted Joel and his family. But because, at one time, she'd thought she was part of Liam's family.

The note only served as a reminder that she'd never belonged anywhere except with her grandparents. And, at least in the case with Liam, she'd been desperate to belong somewhere. She'd been blind to his true personality.

Joel reached over and took her hand in his. The gentle pressure of his palm against hers slowed the angry pounding of her heart.

This was different. Joel was different.

They pulled into the driveway. He lifted their hands to place a kiss against her wrist before letting go. He jogged around to open the door for her.

Anna smiled her thanks.

The front porch light was on and waiting to illuminate their way through the darkness. Epic was in the backyard and barked as soon as he heard their arrival.

The house — the light, her dog, the people waiting inside — all beckoned to Anna like a warm blanket on a cold day.

She followed Joel up the driveway.

Anna yelped in pain when someone grabbed her by the hair and jerked her head back.

Liam!

Laughter filled her ears.

She struggled when she saw Joel turn and approach them.

"Don't come any closer." Liam waved a gun. "I will shoot her and not think twice about it."

Anna stomped hard on his foot, hoping he'd loosen his hold. Instead, Liam used the butt of his gun and slammed it into the side of her head.

White-hot pain flashed behind her eyes. For long moments, she couldn't see a thing. Liam tightened his hold on her hair. When her eyesight cleared, all she saw was the black sky above her.

Cold metal touched her cheek.

Liam's voice boomed in her ear, her head pounding with the noise. Something sticky flowed down her face near the corner of her mouth. "Get back!" He sidestepped further away from the door and towards the driveway. "I will kill her."

"Please, don't hurt them." Anna's voice was breathless even to her own ears. "They've done nothing to deserve your anger, Liam. Leave them alone." Her scalp screamed in response to his continued pulling of her hair.

Liam loosened his hold on her hair long enough to snake an arm around and across her neck. It wasn't hard enough to choke her, but panic rose higher in Anna's chest. Through tear-filled eyes, she identified Chess and Brooke on the front porch. Brooke had a phone to her ear. The police.

Please, God. Please keep us safe. Send help.

Chess had his gun trained on Liam. But with Anna in front, she knew he wasn't going to get a shot off.

Epic's barking became frantic. Loyal dog that he was, she heard him scratching at the wood, trying to get through the fence.

Liam lowered his voice to a raspy whisper. "You'd risk your life to save these people who'll only kick you to the curb in another week or two? Did you think you could run off to some hick town and get away with it?"

Goosebumps peppered her skin. Her mind raced as she struggled against his grasp. With his arm across her throat, she couldn't have responded if she wanted to.

Anna tried to grab for anything within reach. Liam took that free arm and twisted it hard behind her. Tears of pain stung her eyes and slid down her cheeks. She took in deep gasps of air now that her airway was no longer constricted.

"Tell me, *love*, where is my thumb drive?" He spat the words out with such anger that Anna wondered if there'd be any way out of this situation with her life.

She tried to focus on Joel's face and calm her

breathing.

Liam bellowed, "Where is it?!"

Anna's breathing increased. "They don't have it. It's not even in the house. Let me go, and I'll take you to it."

"Do you think I'm stupid?" He shoved the gun into her cheek and she tasted blood. "You tell me where that drive is or I will end you and your friends right now."

Epic continued to bark and tear at the fencing.

Joel took several steps towards Liam despite the objections from his family behind him. The situation was escalating. He could tell by the way Liam was holding Anastasia — the wild look in his eyes.

The combination of the porch light and the blood streaming from her temple appeared to distort Anastasia's face. Her eyes slid shut and her knees buckled.

Without mercy, Liam twisted her arm behind her, bringing her back to her feet. The movement shot an arrow of fear right into Joel's heart.

Joel took another two steps towards them. Liam moved the gun from Anastasia and pointed it at him. Good, that's exactly what he wanted.

"Back up. Or I'll shoot her right now." Liam's powerful voice reached Joel from across the driveway. Liam laughed. "Not that it's any loss. I'd do it anyway if I didn't need that drive. She owes me."

"She owes you nothing, Liam. Let her go." Joel pointed a finger at him. "You kill her, and you go down for murder. Is that what you want?"

Liam only laughed harder. "Don't pretend you've got any amount of control over this situation." He moved the gun back to Anastasia's head.

Dear God, protect her.

Chess approached, stopping when he was shoulder-to-shoulder with Joel. He kept his gun up and trained on Liam.

"Please." Anastasia's pleading broke Joel's heart. "The drive's on Epic's collar. In a cylinder."

Liam's eyes widened and his gaze flitted to the gate right behind him. His face morphed. "I should have known. I'll kill that mutt of yours."

The anticipation of finally getting what he'd come all this way for took Liam's attention off of Anastasia. His grip on her loosened. Joel saw the look in her eyes at the same time she lifted her feet and dropped out of Liam's grasp.

Joel was already running full speed. He was in the air when the deafening sound of the gun collided with a pain in his shoulder.

Before Chess had a chance to return fire, a flurry of white leaped over the fence, slamming into Liam. The gun clattered to the pavement as Liam screamed and the dog snarled.

Epic was moving so quickly it was difficult to tell what was going on. The blood-curdling screams coming from Liam along with the dog's snarls left little to the imagination. All Joel knew was that he needed to get Anastasia out of there.

"Anastasia!" He pulled her into his arms and rolled with her away from the mass of flying teeth and fur.

He covered her body with his own and watched as Chess kicked the gun away from Liam. The man's screams intensified.

Joel felt Anastasia's chest rise as the air filled her lungs. The movement was comforting. She was going to be okay.

Chess kept his gun on Liam. "Anna, call Epic off."

Anastasia's first attempt was barely above a whisper. She took a long breath and Joel could feel her gain strength. "Epic." Another breath. "Epic! That's enough. Come here, buddy."

Joel didn't think Epic had heard her, but he pulled back. Growling, he moved away from Liam.

Chess stepped in. "Turn over and put your hands on the ground above your head."

Liam struggled in an attempt to obey. Even from Joel's position, the blood on the man's face and shirt was visible. There were splatters across Epic's white face as well.

The sounds of sirens filled the air.

Joel struggled to get to his feet, pulling Anastasia gently with him. "Chess? Brooke?"

"We're okay." Chess ran towards them, Brooke right behind him.

Joel's feet went out from under him and he didn't understand why. It wasn't until he propped his shoulder against the side of the house that he realized what had happened.

Liam had shot him in the shoulder. The adrenaline was wearing off and pain sped through his chest and down his left arm.

Three police cars lit the street up with their red and blue lights as officers poured out and quickly took over custody of Liam. Chess slid his gun into its holster and moved to help Joel. "We need a doctor over here. My friend's been shot!"

Joel watched as Brooke ran to Anastasia's side, holding a hand to the wound on her head that continued to ooze blood. Epic didn't leave her. Anastasia didn't seem to be concerned about herself. Instead, she pulled away from Brooke and put a hand on Joel's chest.

"No, no, no!"

Horror and fear flashed across her face.

Was the porch light going out? Why was her face getting darker?

You're safe now, Anastasia.

It was the last thing that went through his mind before the darkness crowded in.

Anna watched as Joel's eyelids lowered and his head fell forward. Two EMTs from the ambulance that had just pulled up rushed to his side.

Brooke held her arm even as Anna tried to get closer to Joel. "Give them room to work, Anna."

Anna stumbled and Chess scooped her up into his arms. She squinted against the lights coming from a fire engine and a second ambulance. Moisture traveled down her face and dripped off her chin. She had no idea if it was tears or blood. Probably a combination.

She craned her neck, keeping her eyes on Joel. Searching for a sign that he was okay. That he was still alive.

"I have to go back, Chess. I need to be with Joel."

Chess tightened his hold on her as he settled her

on a gurney that seemed to appear from nowhere. "I know. But Joel would want me to make sure I got you taken care of. You're hurt, too, Anna." She barely heard his words and struggled to stand back up. Chess finally crouched to her level, blocking her view of Joel. "He will never forgive me if I let something else happen to you. Please, let them take care of you like they're taking care of Joel."

She held still as another EMT shined a light in her eyes, making her brain throb against her skull.

Please, God. Please let Joel be okay. I don't want to let him go. I just found him.

Epic started to jump up beside her but the EMT held a hand out to stop him.

Chess glared at the EMT. "Let the dog be."

The EMT's eyes widened. As if he sensed what had happened, Epic jumped onto the gurney with ease and settled with his chin in Anna's lap.

She focused on Chess. "How's Joel? Is he…?" Her voice sounded breathless even to her own ears.

"He's alive, Anna."

Relief flooded through her body and she slumped. The EMT caught her. "Are you dizzy, miss?"

A thought crossed her mind and her eyes flew open. "Liam?"

Chess gently squeezed her arm. "The police have him in custody. He's a mess." He reached over and scratched Epic's head. "I'm buying this guy here a steak when this is all over."

She let her forehead rest against Chess's shoulder. The ebbing adrenaline left her shaking as if she had no control over her body.

The EMT spoke from behind her. "We're going to

need to bring you in and make sure there's no internal damage as a result of that laceration on your head."

Anna moved her hand to her head, surprised by how much sticky blood there was. Pain from the contact made her nauseated.

One ambulance left. She strained to catch a view of Joel but he was nowhere to be found. Was he on his way to the hospital?

Brooke's voice reached her ears. "Anna, I'm going to take care of Epic for you."

Anna thought she nodded. The EMT helped her lie down on the stretcher. By the time the back of her head touched the fabric, she was falling into blissful unconsciousness.

Chapter Twenty-Three

Voices were the first thing Anna registered. They sounded muffled, yet all around her, at the same time. She struggled to focus her mind and figure out where the sound was originating from.

"I hate every minute of this." That was Brooke. "One of us should be in there. I don't want him to be alone."

Chess's deep voice came from somewhere. "There's nothing we can do about that right now. We'll make sure someone's there when he wakes up."

Anna felt something cold against the back of her right hand.

Mustering all of her strength, she forced her heavy eyelids open and squinted against the daylight coming through the window. Even with the sheer coverings, it seemed as though the sun itself was peeking through the panes.

Anna licked her lips and tried to sit. Muscles in

her midsection and arms cramped in response. Her head pounded, sending waves of nausea through her. She groaned.

Chess came into view quickly followed by Brooke. She put a hand on Anna's shoulder and shook her head. "Don't try to move."

Chess smiled at her. "Welcome back."

Confusion clouded her thoughts. Where was Joel? Scenes from the house flashed through her head like painful movie clips. Liam hitting her with the gun, Joel charging forward to protect her, the image of him slumping forward. It all crashed into her at once, leaving her gasping.

She realized the cold sensation had been the saline going into her body through the IV in the back of her hand. "Is Joel okay?" The words sounded gravelly to her own ears.

Chess gave a single dip of his chin. "He's in surgery. The bullet did significant damage to the nerves and bone in his left shoulder. But he's alive and the doctor hopes that he'll be able to repair the tissue."

Anna let her head fall back against the pillow and moaned when pain pulsed through her. It was her fault Joel was hurt. What was he going to do if he couldn't use his arm again? "Are you two okay?"

"We're fine." Brooke gave her a smile of reassurance.

Anna tried to swallow again. "What time is it?"

"It's after ten in the morning. You've been sleeping for hours." Brooke's eyes flitted to the monitor. "How are you? Should I get a nurse?"

Anna shook her head. "No. I don't need a nurse. I'm not sure yet." She winced as she shifted her position. "I'm thirsty."

Chess straightened. "I'll get you something. Don't go anywhere."

She smiled. Or at least she thought about it. She wasn't entirely sure it had manifested into a real one. She let her eyelids close again and didn't open them until she heard footsteps coming into the room. Chess approached with a clear plastic cup of water closely flanked by a nurse. He handed the cup to Brooke. "Sorry. She insisted on coming when I asked for the water."

Brooke helped Anna take two sips before setting the cup on a tray near the bed. She backed up while the nurse examined Anna, asked more questions than she could remember, and wrote everything in her medical chart.

"When can I get out of here? I need to be there when Joel wakes up."

The nurse checked her vitals patiently. "You've got a pretty serious concussion and it took eight stitches to close that laceration. The doctor is making his rounds. But I guarantee you're not going anywhere until you are able to sit without vomiting."

Anna wanted to argue. But when she moved and thought she was going to lose the contents of her stomach, she knew the nurse was right. Even if she hated it.

The nurse made a final note in the charts and left. Anna took in a lungful of air. She closed her eyes against the brightness of the room. Her mind went over the events of the night before. "Where's Epic?"

It was Chess who answered that question. "Epic is fine. He's staying at a kennel with a vet until you're back on your feet. He ended up with cuts on his paws from climbing over that fence to help you. I spoke with the vet this morning and he said they'll heal nicely. He had a hand in saving the day, Anna."

She thought about her faithful friend and tears flooded her eyes. If Epic hadn't acted when he did...

All sorts of images and thoughts rushed through her head. Nightmares. She tried to shake them away.

Thank God Epic was okay.

But what about Joel? He'd gotten shot to protect her. He had to be okay. *God, let him be okay.*

She opened her eyelids a crack. "Have we received any updates on what they're going to do with Liam?"

Chess stepped forward. "He's behind bars, Anna. We're going to make sure he stays there for a very long time."

Good. That was good. "I wish we'd gotten access to those files, though. If we had, we could add embezzlement to the list of charges."

Brooke grinned and reached into her pocket. "I got the thumb drive from Epic before I left the vet's office."

Chess stepped forward and held something up. "And I happened to find this on the ground by Liam before the police took him away."

"It's the key code, Anna," Brooke verified. "We've got the files."

For the first time since she'd awakened, Anna smiled. "You guys are amazing." She yawned. "I think I'm going to get some rest. That's a sure-fire way to get the doctor to show up sooner rather than later, right?"

"Definitely." Brooke laid a hand on Anna's. "You

sure you don't need anything?"

"Wake me up when Joel's out of surgery. I want to know how he's doing."

"We will."

Anna's eyelids slid down again. Her thoughts centered on Joel.

It was Liam's fault Joel was hurt. His insanity led him to pull that trigger.

But if she'd stayed and faced him in Utah — or if she'd kept moving instead of trying to settle in Quintin... Well, it was because of her that Joel was in surgery now. He'd stepped in the way of that bullet — saved her life.

What if he didn't regain full use of his arm? What if he blamed her?

What if, after all of this, she lost her new family like Liam said she would?

Suddenly exhausted, and on the verge of tears, Anna tried to banish the thoughts to the far recesses of her mind. A single tear escaped and slid down her cheek and she welcomed the sleep that claimed her.

When Anna awoke again, her brain was much faster to respond. The room seemed full of voices. When she opened her eyes, she found one doctor taking her vitals and checking the laceration on her head.

Meanwhile, another doctor — clearly a surgeon — spoke to the others.

"Joel is out of surgery. We wheeled him into recovery. The procedure was successful and I was able to repair the damage to his humerus as well as the tissue surrounding it. He's in stable condition." The surgeon paused. "He is going to need to go through extensive physical therapy with that arm. I'm hopeful that he'll get to the point where he has full strength again. But it won't be easy."

"How long will Joel be hospitalized?" asked Brooke.

"I can't say for certain until he wakes up and we see how he does. My best guess is that he'll need to remain here for a couple of days and then you'll be able to take him home. We'll be bringing him to a room right down the hall as soon as he's able to leave recovery."

Anna's attention moved from him to the doctor examining her. "I need to be there when Joel wakes up." She surprised herself with the steadiness of her own voice. She noted his nametag. "Doctor Terrance. I'll be there if my friends have to wheel me in like this."

The doctor chuckled as Chess and Brooke moved to stand around her bed. "I believe that you would, too." He held a hand out to her. "I want you to try sitting up. Are you ready?"

She nodded and he slowly raised the bed until she was upright. Her head pounded and nausea still pulsed through her, but it was nothing like she felt before.

Doctor Terrance gave a satisfied grunt. "You've been given pain medication as well as medication to help with the nausea. You've received a nasty concussion. It's very important that you take it easy. I want you to stay here at least overnight so we can monitor you." He jotted a few things down on her chart. "But I don't see why you all can't go sit with your friend once he's brought down here." He gave her a small smile and then cleared his throat. He pointed a finger at her. "You ride in a wheelchair and that IV stays in place until tomorrow. Agreed?"

"Agreed." Anna took in a steadying breath. "Thank you, doctor."

"I'll be back first thing in the morning to check on you again. Ring for the nurse if you need anything. You can eat and drink as you're up to it. Don't rush things. It's going to take a while to recover."

Anna nodded and regretted the movement. She turned to say something but Chess spoke before she had the chance.

"I'll talk to the nurse about having a wheelchair brought in to make sure you're ready as soon as they give us the word."

Anna let her body relax against the hospital bed. She took in the relieved faces of the people around her.

"Thank you both. After everything I've put you through, you didn't have to be here with me."

Brooke's eyebrows shot up in surprise. "Are you kidding me? Where else would we be? Joel would kill us if we didn't keep an eye on you right now while he wasn't able to."

But it was Chess who pierced her with an expression that left her no doubt he spoke for the others when he said, "You're family. We aren't going anywhere."

Tears flooded Anna's eyes. But for the first time in a long while, they weren't tears of pain or sadness.

Chapter Twenty-Four

Joel fought to untangle the mess of dreams and reality flowing through his head. He watched, helpless, as Liam hit Anastasia with the butt of his gun. Blood dribbled down her face, marring the whiteness of her skin.

That red river. It was all he saw. He groaned, heat and pain spreading through his left shoulder and into his chest.

The sound of a gunshot made him jump. The relief of having Anastasia in his arms.

And then darkness.

Where was he? Was Anastasia okay?

Why wouldn't his blasted eyelids open?

Frustrated with himself, he groaned. That was when he felt something touch his arm.

"Joel? Can you hear me?"

"Hey, man. You're in the hospital."

Using every ounce of effort he had, Joel forced his eyes open. Blinking several times to clear the fog, he focused on the faces observing him.

Chess standing near the foot of his bed, a relieved smile on his face. Brooke on one side, her eyes bright with unshed tears.

And Anastasia. She was watching him, worry etched into her features. He realized she was sitting in a wheelchair, an IV bag hanging from a pole nearby. A white bandage on her forehead stood in stark contrast to her hair.

He lifted his right hand to caress her cheek. "Are you okay?"

"Thanks to you," she whispered.

"Praise God." He winced when pain traveled through his shoulder. He let his eyes close for what he thought was a moment. But when he opened them again, the room was dark. How much time had passed?

There was pressure against his right shoulder and it was only then that he realized Anastasia was bent over, her arms crossed on the bed beside him. Her head was resting there, one hand hovering over his.

Brooke appeared from the other side. She smiled. "Anna refused to leave your side. She's been asleep like that for over an hour."

He moved his thumb enough to rub the soft skin on her wrist. "Is she going to be all right?" He whispered, not wanting to wake Anastasia.

"Yeah. The doctor said she has a concussion. She'll probably get released tomorrow."

"Where's Chess?" Joel tried to take in the room but wasn't too successful.

"He's trying to catch a few hours of sleep out in the waiting room. This little couch I'm on wasn't big enough for him."

Joel tried to picture Chess curled up on the small piece of furniture and chuckled. He groaned, wishing he hadn't.

Anastasia stirred and raised her head slowly. "Hey. You're awake again." She rubbed her eyes with one of her hands.

Joel cleared his throat and Brooke helped him get a drink of water.

Brooke smiled. "Tell you what. I seriously need a cup of coffee. Why don't I give you two a few minutes?"

Anastasia's gaze followed Brooke as she left the room before resting on him. She had creases on one of her cheeks from sleeping. Her hair was disheveled, surrounding her face like a halo.

She was the prettiest thing he'd ever seen.

He smiled. "I'm amazed you convinced them to let you stay in here." He realized she was still in the wheelchair.

Dimples came to life. "Let's just say I didn't leave them much of a choice." She sobered. "I'm sorry for what happened to you." Her voice broke and a tear escaped, leaving a glistening trail behind it. She brushed it away. "I wish..."

Joel tried to sit and clenched his fist in frustration when he wasn't able to. "Don't. Look at me, Anastasia." She did as several more tears fell. "I'm not remotely sorry. The nightmare you've been living for months is over. You're safe."

"But your arm!"

"I still have it." He shifted and groaned again. "Trust me, I know it's still there. I can feel it throbbing."

She chuckled through her tears.

Her laughter did a world of good for Joel's heart. "I'm going to be fine. It's going to heal. And if not? Well, I'm pretty sure I can fix a burger one-handed." He winked at her and was rewarded with another little laugh.

Anastasia used both of her hands to wipe away her tears. She sniffed. Then, as if she realized what she must look like, her hands flew to her hair. She used her fingers to rake the strands into some semblance of order.

"You are beautiful. Always."

She ducked her chin and when she raised it again, a smile lit up her face.

"Thanks for believing in me, Joel. For saving my life."

Joel exhaled. "I wish I could hold you right now."

"Me, too."

He raised his hand to her face and gently guided her towards him. Their lips touched briefly before she laid her head on his good shoulder. He groaned. "That kiss was...painful."

Anastasia shook with laughter then cradled her head with her hands. "It sure was." She lifted her chin, mischief glittering in her eyes. "But it was worth it."

"Oh yeah."

Three weeks later…

Anna stood with one shoulder leaning against the wooden fence in her backyard. The April sun sank below the horizon, leaving a sea of amber clouds in its wake.

She heard the back door open. Moments later, a muscular arm came around her waist. She breathed in Joel's woodsy aftershave as it drifted to her on the spring breeze.

"Did you just get here?" she asked.

"Yep. As quick as I could. I knew Brooke wasn't going to hold movie night for me much longer."

Anna relaxed against his chest, her eyes still on the rapidly-changing sky. "I wish you'd waited another week before going back to work. And I should have insisted on helping you close the diner tonight." She should be thankful he'd agreed to wait another month before going forward with plans to open the diner for breakfast.

"I'm fine. You know sitting around my house is driving me crazy."

"Oh, Chess has been telling us all about it tonight." She tried to contain her laughter. By the way he tightened his arm around her waist, he heard it.

"I'll bet he has." He kissed her cheek and settled his chin on her shoulder. "What are you still doing out here?" His voice was husky as he spoke near her ear.

Goosebumps traveled up Anna's arm. She motioned towards the clouds. "Pretty, isn't it?"

"The second prettiest thing I've seen tonight."

Anna's breath caught. He loosened his hold and she turned to face him. "You're sweet."

"You make it easy." He kissed the tip of her nose. "How's your evening been since I last saw you?"

"I got the call we've been waiting for." She

bounced on her toes and grinned. "The investigators not only tied the agency fire to Liam, but all the evidence needed to prove he embezzled money from his own company was on that thumb drive. Add in the attempted murder and they're putting him away for a very long time."

Joel hugged her to him. "I'm glad. Though that's too good for him, if you ask me." His eyes traveled to her forehead and the wound that was still visible. He lightly ran a finger over the scar. Epic barked. "See, he agrees with me."

Anna shook her head in amusement. "We'd better go inside. Brooke's probably getting impatient. We're messing with the movie start time."

"She'll survive." Joel dipped his head and captured Anna's lips with his.

She melted into his embrace as he kissed every last thought from her mind. They were here together. That's all that mattered.

Brooke's voice carried through the backdoor. "You two want to come up for air and get your butts in here sometime tonight?"

Anna let her forehead rest against his chest which shook with laughter.

Joel waited until Brooke disappeared. His lips brushed against her ear. "I love you."

"I love you, too." Warmth flooded her heart and traveled to every cell in her body.

"Give it to God, Anna. He'll see you through."

Grandma had been right. Anna shook her head in amazement as she thought about the way God protected her and brought her here.

Joel put an arm around Anna's shoulders and

hugged her close. He led her back to the house and the rest of the family.

Their family.

About the Author

Melanie D. Snitker has enjoyed writing fiction for as long as she can remember. She started out writing episodes of cartoon shows that she wanted to see as a child and her love of writing grew from there. She and her husband live in Texas with their two children who keep their lives full of adventure, and two dogs who add a dash of mischief to the family dynamics. In her spare time, Melanie enjoys photography, reading, crochet, baking, archery, camping, and hanging out with family and friends.

http://www.melaniedsnitker.com
https://twitter.com/MelanieDSnitker
https://www.facebook.com/melaniedsnitker

Acknowledgments

Doug, Xander, and Sydney, I can never express how much the three of you mean to me. I love you!

Crystal, thank you so much for helping me work out the plot. It was a big undertaking and if it hadn't been for your help, I'm pretty sure I'd have gone insane. I learned a lot through this process. Here's hoping the next one will be less of a challenge.

Victorine, thank you for letting me talk through the suspense thread. Your insight was very helpful. And, as always, the cover is beautiful!

I appreciate the wonderful members of my critique group: Franky, Rachel, Victorine, and Crystal. I couldn't do this without you.

Steph, Melissa, Denny, Sandy, Doug, Mom (Suzanne), CeeCee, Faith, and Shanna, as my beta readers, you play a big role in this process. I'm very thankful for you!

Most importantly, I want to thank my Heavenly Father for all of His many blessings. My cup runneth over.

Other Books by Melanie D. Snitker

Calming the Storm
(A Christian Romance Novel)

Love's Compass Series:
Finding Peace (Book 1)
Finding Hope (Book 2)
Finding Courage (Book 3)
Finding Faith (Book 4)

Life Unexpected Series:
Safe In His Arms (Book 1)

Made in the USA
Columbia, SC
10 December 2017